BLACK MACABRE, VOLUME 1

THANKING EVIL

BLACK MACABRE VOL.1
THANKING EVIL

URAL GARRETT

OVER THE EDGE BOOKS

los angeles

Book Design by Lily J. Noonan

Published by Over the Edge Books, Los Angeles

www.overtheedgebooks.com

Thanking Evil: Black Macabre Volume 1/Ural Garrett—1st ed.
ISBN 978-1-944082-16-1 (print), ISBN 978-1-944082-17-8 (digital)

Dedicated to those who
pray for my death daily.

Prologue

Grandmother always used the story of God and Satan as some sick twisted tale of obedience. You know that heavenly choir director who decides he doesn't want to be a follower any more? Ends up taking a loss and becomes destined to live an eternity of damnation.

Well guess what? I've seen enough of the world not to blame him for trying. We live in a constant maze, desperately attempting to find life's purpose while surviving reality. My existence shouldn't be this bleak. Those first steps into adulthood are creeping around the corner; yesterday was high school graduation.

I don't know much about the future. Grades, money: neither warrant much hope...or pussy. That was until a strange email entered my inbox with a subject line that read: Your Way Out.

Inside was a hyperlink to a community that altered my future. That link led to URL after URL and finally landing at an old message board with only one thread that was created by a user named LaVey667. Inside the post was a download link to a PDF file.

Past the deaths of my parents, the world I inhabit offers nothing better than the dark side of purgatory. Now I could have something that gives me the illusion of real power. Illusions that will finally grant me the ability to erase those who have not only ruined me but my family. They ruined my existence and they will be removed from this physical plane. One by one, those tasting other worldly revenge will surely understand my suffering.

But first I have to make sure this shit works because this could all be some type of hoax. At worst, I fuck up the floor with this charcoal, set some shit on fire, and continue to live in the depths of obscurity. Funny how the human spirit sometimes finds hope in the most evil things. Hell, we're all just animals at the core, right? Maybe it's time for my monstrosity to be unleashed.

Step One: Drawing a pentagram takes time and patience. At least that's what the PDF document on the Thanking Evil message board alluded to. Thankfully I drew an outline on the carpet with my own blood beforehand. Guess we can all agree that turning back is not an option. Smoldering hot charcoal only adds to the mess. Photos of my past and present are set on fire with a nearby Bic lighter. I got it right though. A few candles from Botanica Obatala subtly light the room enough for me to read the just barely legible Latin passage:

Plurimum enim Satan. Per legatos petit, reverenter, potentiam tuam, et tua disperdes inimicos meos.

(Translation: There is the great Satan. Through the ambassadors we ask reverently that thy might destroy my enemies.)

The project walls swell, warp, and shake. Books and a lamp fall violently from a nearby desk, squashing a roach that may be pregnant, as a small egg shaped pill shoots from its abdomen. As the room fills with strange hues of crimson amber, the only thing visible is the light on this fairly old netbook running Windows XP before blacking out. There I lay; limp with blood pouring from every orifice. The instructions required my nudity and the fuzzy cheap carpet couldn't have been colder that night. My chest burned as I inhaled the smells of rotten eggs and death. Oh shit, it's sulfur. Looks like things are looking up.

The smell remains when I awake to a cathedral filled with the same crimson amber. The first thing visible is an upside down cross floating over what looked to be a pulpit. Screeching and thunder sonically contrast every dissonant harp string, hitting all the right notes.

Silk overlays a plush floor as I place one sole in front of the other, inching closer to a woman who looks too good to be an angel. Naw, she's better. Gold adorned her fingers and toes. To say she had a coke bottle figure sounds lazy and cliché. Her breasts couldn't have been more perfect. From my vantage point, I could have slept for seven eternities on them.

Damn, it was almost as if she was sculpted by someone with sinister plans.

Never in a million millennia would I believe such elegance was in store. Laying my eyes on her pink matter was the first moment I gazed upon life itself. Her facial features are more refined. Couldn't tell if she was black, white, or something in-between. Man, those jade colored eyes of hers were filled with lust, dread, and mystery. French braids covered horns that pointed up toward the heavens like a spiritual middle finger. *Would she be put off if she saw my dick hard?* Officially in her presence, I became harder than geese erection. She moves to me and touches me in ways not discussed by the jocks in the locker room, pushing me forcefully on my back. Even underneath, the view couldn't have been more amazing.

Hands reached from beneath the textured material and hold me in place for an experience unknown to me. She straddles me, slowly kissing me with passion. I'm hers. Watching her long, forked tongue circle around those red lips of hers further excited me. This wasn't just a beautiful demonic figure teasing the greatest, and probably singular, sexual experience of my life. No, the books didn't tell me about this part of the ritual that included putting that mouth to work after tracing her tongue down my abdomen.

Still held in place firmly by those soft hands, she faces me after forcing me down her throat. By then, I began to understand the power between those thighs. Those hips rocked and swayed me into a far away dimension. My hands were free enough to grab her Venetian comforter-soft posterior. That's the shit rappers talk about in their rhymes. Too much and I would explode into a million pieces. Wait, I did explode. Breathing heavily, like the one time I ran from some stick-up men looking for their day's meal, wasn't the only indication that the ritual was complete.

Fear set in almost instantly. The once cherubic face decays into something terrifying. Finally opening her mouth to speak, only four words are recited: "You have three days," she says in a baritone reverb. Decomposing to the bone, her head falls unto my face as I awaken in the same room, home to me since moving in with Momma Smith, several years past moments when life gave me one nasty fuck you.

Was it one helluva dream? Or was it real? Covered in blood and charcoal from last night, I feel like shit regardless, so something must have happened.

It's early morning, and I feel as if getting hit by a Tyson Chicken truck couldn't describe this pain. I almost can't move. A nearby alarm clock reveals 5 o'clock AM. Looking downward, something is also moving in my stomach. Whatever entity occupying my digestive system forces me to find the nearest trashcan. No, that isn't last night's ramen noodles. What the fuck? Blood, maggots and snake scales? This ain't normal. Then again, what just transpired wasn't either. My end is near, but before the time comes, many will be punished. Oblivion is at hand.

Chapter One

My tastebuds have changed. My mouth feels as if I've spent the last few days snacking on rusted shower-heads. Was the previous night worth it? Who knows? Holding out my hand and thinking about moving a nearby chair yields no results. Man, this is bullshit. All this mess for nothing. Back to my personal hell. And to think, I have work in a couple of hours. Well, I'm already nude. Might as well go hop in the shower, brush my teeth, and get dressed.

Standing there naked in front of the bathroom's body length mirror hanging from the door, I noticed my 5'9" stature grew a few inches. The black as oil complexion grew darker and looked better than before. My face didn't look like a crater either. The lankiness turned into a slight ripped muscular frame. Looking further below, my dick got bigger, too.

So there we have it, ladies and gentleman, a fantastic early morning start. Let me go take care of Momma Smith's daily pills and breakfast since I'll be gone for a nice slice of the day. Cozaar for her hypertension, Stadol for back pain; you know, the easy stuff. But making sure she has the right dosage of Granisetron for nausea caused by the radiation treatments becomes tricky every now and then. Just in case she gets the urge to throw up, I have a freshly cleaned pan that's cleaned every night. Overall, cooking was never my forte, but my packaged Quaker Oaks can outdo Julia Child and that's a fact. Plus, that was all she could hold in anyway. At least I have a win there.

With that task complete, time to head to my 9-5: HD Chicken. Before I go, a small peck on those once-rosy cheeks almost feels like a worthless exercise in good luck. She's still sleeping so I'll leave the good-byes and love you stuff alone. Something tells me if no one else understands this heart of mine, she does.

Located around five blocks east from my crib, HD Chicken was the only place hiring. Being honest, the only reason I probably got the job was my lack of felonies and tattoos. Guess knowing basic addition and subtraction is a rarity these days. For the past year and a half, I've evolved from customer service representative to Fry Tech, or the nigga that makes french fries. It's a shitty job but helps pay a few bills and Momma Smith's meds.

Though the establishment doesn't open until 11 AM, my shift starts a few hours earlier for early prep. Getting chicken properly seasoned with prepackaged herbs, making sure all the pre-prepared sides are heated, and biscuits, packed with more unpronounceable chemicals than store-bought roach spray, are cooked to perfection in less than ten minutes. Hood fried chicken spots don't get this grimy. Customers don't make things any better. Some could say working fast food means being the last step in absorbing emotional baggage brought on by the world. Employment opportunities like these aren't about learning new skills and growth; they're a test in how thick-skinned one is. Matter of fact, the job description should simply say, "Verbal punching bag." But with my life story so far, it's become the least of my annoyances.

Today also happens to be grease trap cleanout day, per the job calendar. The back door, facing a dirty alley reeking of broken dreams, crack pipes, and urine, was already open as a large suction tube stretched to a nearby truck collecting the oily debris. Several feet to the right of the rear entrance is the office of my manager, Johnny D. There was always a nervousness that hit my stomach every time I walked past it on my way to clock out. Johnny D was something worse than an asshole. Mid-forties and nowhere to go, his position gave him a small sense of power that made him a sinister figure. The nigga was round as fuck with a creepy baritone voice. Some around the place called him the hood Jabba the Hutt.

At the start, I just tolerated him for his cruel way of turning everyone against each other through promises of raises and time off. Things went from bad to worse when I turned down a promotion that only upped my meager minimum wage rate by 20 cents. Since then, he just likes to fuck with me.

That continues as I almost almost finish punching in my employee code and password to clock in before he wobbles his ass over to say, "Don't worry about clocking in today, Patcher," as the stench of bunk and early morning Hennessy flows from his lipsmouth. "Labor is already high and I have to train Quesha today. She's the new assistant manager."

Normally, I would have taken that level of disrespect with a grain of salt. Something came over me and whispered into the depths of my id: *Not today.*

The oval-shaped man's hatred of me must have been a decades-long wish for revenge. Him, Mom and Dad all went to the same high school way back. Apparently, his first girlfriend (who became my mother) Naomi left him for my father after he got caught dicking down his fair share of hoes. Doesn't help that a later arrest for rape destroyed his chances at the pros. Some could say that every look into my brown eyes reminded him of everything he lost. Dropping me from the schedule minutes before I arrive and missed opportunities of advancement after promises all gave him a sense of purpose. Torment the living representation of his life's failures. Too bad he didn't realize that their relationship didn't last too long then either. But Mother and Father would get reunited later.

"Wonder how much semen Quesha had to swallow considering she lacks a high school diploma, which is a requirement for the position," I retorted with a confidence I didn't realize was there. Johnny D was taken aback more than I was.

Regaining his composure quickly, he fired back. "She swallowed well enough to replace ya ass tomorrow. Since you want to be a smart ass, don't worry about showing up the day after either."

Then something along the lines of "Fuck yo' Weeble Wobble ass, nigga," spits from my mouth so autonomously. *Shit, that felt good.*

Then it hit me. *Well damn, the shit might have worked.* No fire shooting out of my hands. No super strength. A nigga not even flying and shit. As visions of last night's dreams flash into my thoughts, I realize the only thing that came from the ordeal was a backbone. But growing a pair of balls felt good enough.

Snapping back into the moment I hear, "Ah fuck me? Ha! You can hand in your badge and apron. Don't worry about coming back."

I sink into myself and realize I fucked up. Money for bills and medication was thrown out of the window. The fuck was I to do? At least I had enough stored for Momma Smith until a month from now. My lips crack a smile before calmly speaking in my normal voice, "That's fine. I'll be back for my check tomorrow."

Exiting the rear door and hopping gleefully over the suction tube, the large fuckboy yells, "Ya bitch ass check will be here at three." Making my way home for another job search can serve as a healthy reminder of life's expendable possibilities.

A walk past a small local park is on my route back to the dilapidated project building. Small children play around in the cesspool of a sandbox that's lightly sprinkled with used condoms, needles, and various body fluids. No worries for them yet. I miss those times. Watching their offspring smile in delight, mothers converse about today's topics on everything including stories of infidelity, murder, and triumphs, big or small. Or, whatever was available on MediaTakeout viewable from their cheaply made pre-paid smartphones.

Nearby, street pharmacists serve the dope fiends without a care in the world of their impact—at least on the exterior. Paranoia internally becomes torment with every thought of jail time. A life-ending hollow point can show up at any precious moment. But for now, the only thing that matters is making money and evading the more respectable cops. Crooked ones can get paid off if they don't kill you. Some deal hopes of money and bitches as a recruitment tactic. Those without hope giving false hope to the future. Normally watching the sight of these games is difficult enough and makes my head to hang down in both fear and disappointment. But today, I watch with fascination.

Interesting transitions between pushing drugs and the occasional pick-up game of basketball occur on the court several feet away from me. The Westside Lord members take place and some watch their brothers' backs. Their hearts are in each game as if they're preparing for the playoffs. No refs and some rules are broken.

My eyes fixate on a pearl white Dodge Charger with all the hood amenities creeping slowly like a panther anticipating his next meal. I can see the window roll down slowly before the sunshine reflects light from 22-inch-rims and desert eagle's barrel protruding out the front passenger side along with weed smoke. The back driver side window opens with an assault rifle and the war cry of *BGD Bitch!* echoes loud before the destruction.

Shots ring out on the park with bullets knocking down anything in the path. Metal, wood, flesh, bone. My instincts tell me to hit the floor quickly. Almost in slow motion, I can see the chamber slide toward the shooter's eye as gun powder and residue make way for the bullet to pass the barrel. They say bullets have no name. This time, the object's trajectory through that child's chest said differently.

My head rises from being tucked in my chest almost like a turtle. Shots continue like repetitive drum snares with extra bass. I can feel the end of a bullet tearing through my neck and exiting my spine.

A burning sensation comes. I should be dead. I can still move with freedom past the pain. Why am I still alive? Wait, this is more than ill-gotten confidence.

I'm at my feet. The first thing visible is a crowd hovering over a crying mother hugging her lifeless child. "Why my baby?" she howls.

I move past the crowd of onlookers and gaze into her eyes with assurance. She looks into the crowd as if she is about to witness the spectacle of her life.

I press my hand firmly against the boy's chest covered by a bloodied Trunkfit shirt. Before even the police and ambulance arrive, I can see his blood return to his body. The nerve endings and blood vessels reattached to his collapsed lung. Bone fragments reattach to his ribs as the bullet floating through his lung pushes through his healing epidermis. His lungs fill with air and the boy opens his eyes. My first miracle.

Chatter from the perpetrators in the pearl Dodge Charger already zoomed off miles away is humming in my head. Sensory overload has come upon me as I'm drawn to them. Running faster than the speeding bullet that just tried to end this story fairly quickly, I find them in a vacant lot. Weed lingers the air and gets stronger and stronger. The biggest giveaway of their location is the loud bass of 808s and fiercely chopped snares through the aftermarket amplifier.

Walking toward the vehicle, one of the three gang members inside was wearing a long black tee, matching do-rag and a gold grill and asking, "Who the fuck is that walking toward us?"

The homie behind the wheel proclaims with assurance, "Don't know, but if he don't back the fuck up, he will feel this hollow point, my nigga."

But their bravado disappears as I can see the fear in their eyes when I walk closer and they realize they're trapped in the car.

"What the fuck is happening, bruh?" asks the driver while his dreads shake with a rhythm of terror and he shakes at the door handle. The assault rifle toting nigga in the back with the fucked up Boosie fade tries to shoot his way out but his gun is jammed. Their panic is exciting me beyond comfortable levels.

Dread Head and Do-Rag both reach for their respective tools before realizing their guns are jammed as well. They try to turn down the music but can't until they hear my voice through the car's speakers.

"You niggas like bussin' at folks, right? I'm going to do the world a favor and erase your existence. Matter of fact, I'm going to do your dumb ass parents who birthed you a generous favor so they don't have to start a GoFundMe page for your fucking casket."

I can feel power flow through my arm as the three-ton vehicle begins to levitate. You know them niggas in the whip ain't never seen this level of supernatural shit. And to think, their greatest moment would be their last. My open palm corresponds to the car imploding slowly on itself. Their flesh began to meld together with the car components as I close my fist.

Their screams for help are muffled as motor oil, transmission fluid, and wiper fluid mix with all three gang members' blood onto the concrete. When the orb of the all-white compacted vehicle touched the pavement, the grounded remains painted the parts like a freshly popped pimp on a pre-teen close to puberty.

Pow! The orb burst into flames before exploding. Charred bone fragments, skin, teeth, and mostly fake jewelry were their only physical remains. It was a beautiful display of power, and finally last night started to make much more sense.

Topping things off, I was closer to my building. I turned from the scene and began strolling home again. Seeing Momma Smith cheers me up despite her having only months left to live. I enjoy taking care of Granny just as she did for me when I was younger.

Those roles have reversed since the diagnosis last year. Stage 4 lung cancer they said. Shit couldn't have gotten any worse considering the past several years beforehand. Even the lung removal surgery failed to lend any positive results as the disease spread. She always kept her belief in God regardless of the situation. Matter of fact, she kept attending Mount Ebal Baptist Church until her body refused. She would always say, "God's got it." I knew He didn't, but smiling and agreeing managed to always put a smile on her face. Death is an inevitability, leaving the question of only when. The small speck of light within the dark hole of my soul, seeing her could be considered a sole bright spot.

But by the time I made it home, opening the door revealed her lifeless corpse. I can tell her demise by the forest green bile expelled from her mouth to the soaked carpet. A human body's length behind her back was a cheap flip-phone with only one press of the send button needed. Cancer had embraced her fully.

Evil leaves me for a moment so I can embrace the sorrow of seeing her dead.

Since the murder of my mother and father, Granny could be described as a product of a community hell-bent on destroying her, alongside the future she cared about. Only a child when her family fled the Jim Crow-era South, her reasons have transformed or evolved over time. One involved some white men threatening to kill the entire family once rumors of an affair with the mayor's wife became too wide spread. Another involved some stolen cows. Regardless, these stories always ended with a narrow family escape to the North to flee from white folks bent on their favorite creative way of public execution.

Aww, come on now, lynching did exactly what it was suppose to do. The practice both physically and psychologically fucked up black folks and served to always remind them to remain in their place. If the neck snap didn't kill you, the slow and excruciating loss of oxygen was glad to play back-up. Must have been a terrifying experience to watch a loved one struggle for survival that would never come. Blacks were seen as superhuman enough to sometimes not require air. Made sense for them to set us ablaze afterwards as an added insurance policy.

Walking outside to watch a dangling corpse had to be one sight to see. Never completely understood the whole post-mortem castration for prize thing though. Where white folks using our dicks like a war trophy? Well, head scalping of Native Americans probably served the same purpose.

Life didn't get much better after the move with housing discrimination, even more crooked police, and fucked up niggas. Out of the frying pan and into the fire, right? Guess by the time she gave birth to my father, no jobs and crack created a deadly combination that filled the core of my being. Guess that's why my dad was so militant.

Uncle Ronald and his wife Porsche had already prepared for the news. At this point, he was my only living relative who cared even a smidgen. I picked up the flip phone clinging to life itself with only five percent left in power. I call the hospice center who routinely took care of Granny twice or so a week to inform them. Next, I gave Uncle Ronald the news with the last remaining three percent. He already knew.

"She's gone," he said without me saying a word. "Well, I'm going to call the funeral home folks so they can get the body and be on their way," he said slowly. I could physically feel the punch to his guts in hearing something he knew was coming after Granny chose in-home hospice care.

Twenty minutes passed by before Uncle Ronald and his wife Porsche pulled up in their old beat up Eddie Bauer Edition Expedition. Pulling up to the parking lot behind them seconds later is the coroner and folks from a nearby funeral home. Uncle Ronald and Porsche have a discussion as the coroner and two fairly large men in dusty clothes come into the complex to my unit. I welcome them in as they give their condolences.

The coroner reviews her cold corpse with an eagle eye level of detail. She even places her middle and index finger on her neck to check for a pulse as if the obvious wasn't enough. She sits down at the oak table that's older than me, removes a notebook from her oversized purse, and finds a form. This is when the questioning starts.

"What time did you notice she was dead?" she begins. The questions continue, name, date of birth, and so on. "Any medications, you know, like prescribed narcotics that need to be removed?" is her final query to me.

By the time I finish answering, the two men from the funeral home enter with a white body bag. Uncle Ronald and Aunt Porsche follow.

It's just too much to take. I escape to my room as the door almost understands my pain and closes itself after my entrance. I feel myself glow with surefire rage.

Even the sounds of Uncle Ronald pounding on the door asking to enter sound hollow. Being the swell guy he's always been, I could tell he was concerned. The pressures of adult life, alongside the death of his own mother, was the ultimate test of manhood emotions that I'd failed. I can sense he thought

I was in the process of taking my own life. Too bad he didn't realize that already happened. The knocks elevate, attempting to forcefully open the door first by kicking it in. I hear him say, "This shit must be reinforced with steel mane." He seems panicked, but I can't care.

Aunt Porsche, always finding inventive ways to prove herself as his better half, whispers in his ear to give up. "Look, the body is on its way to the funeral home and we have to pick the kids up from school. Plus, you have to get away for a minute. I already called your job and let them know."

This is the first time I hear Uncle Ronald cry since my Dad's funeral. I can almost feel him get up and go to the car.

"Patcher, I understand how you feel. Why don't you come by for a minute later so we can talk?" she says sweetly. The mixture of calmness and hood attitude hums from her mouth with assurance. "You know the County is going to come in a couple of weeks to start the process of moving in a new tenant. We're going to have to figure some things out, alright." I stay silent behind the door. "Well, I'm going to go now. Just call us when you get a chance, please."

I felt spent. Nothing mattered much to me anymore.

Best thing I could do is get some sleep. Aunt Porsche locked the door on her way out. For the first time ever, the apartment felt empty. I'd spent significant years of my development attached to this place. Nothing but ambient silence filled the air. The sounds of rodents scurrying around for crumbs, an ambulance passing by in search of its newest gunshot victim as police sirens wondered for perpetrators. Loud music thumped next door from the families of those without employment attempting to pass the time with Trap Music, weed, MD 20/20, and laughter brought by the latest bootleg DVD.

Tonight's feature presentation, "Tyler Perry Presents: Madea Goes To Hell, The Final Friday." Maybe recording some audio of recent events will keep me from crying myself to sleep on the trusty netbook. If not, rest won't be too hard.

Chapter Two

Saturday
4:48AM

Word spread of Momma Smith's death. Everyone was saddened on the news of Sweet Momma Smith. Before her life turned for the worse, she took care of the neighborhood in small ways. Taking care of women's children when work became a priority, cooking meals for a few stragglers, and her participation within church auxiliaries. Ironically, very few came to visit when shit got real with the cancer. No one cared much. That's fine, by now they know what they lost.

Like urban vultures, the local crackheads were delighted with the opportunity to scrap up whatever they could possibly sell. The fifteen-minute high always needed attention and the trinkets of a 80-year-old woman in the projects couldn't have been considered the mother lode. Awaking to the sounds of these pests poring over what little bit we had woke me from my grieving slumber. I always found it interesting how much a drug could control someone's mind so much. Being bold enough to rob and steal from those with very little takes a level of guts that's almost supernatural.

The cheap LCD clock sitting on top of my nearby nightstand reads 4:48AM. That's two minutes from when the alarm rings. I slowly reach over to quietly switch it off. Shadows dance as light seeps from under the door. *I'm going to kill these two.*

Leaving my bed and approaching the door slowly, the freshly applied WD-40 on my hinges from a few weeks ago canceled creaks as I witnessed one middle-aged man looking for what outlet the television power plug cord led to. The smell of urine, sweat, and disappointment radiated from his pores. The twenty bucks the television would fetch meant euphoria for a longer amount of time. That's all that mattered.

The feeling of success ran from his rotten smile when I quickly grabbed his head hard enough to leave only his spine attached to his body. Dropping his body to the floor, he twitched madly as blood spewed from the various disconnected arteries in his neck. It painted the living room pre-down darkness. He didn't even scream.

"Yo, Thomas," a high-pitched voice calls with a dusty cadence. "I got everything up over here that I could so we can hurry up and sell it. You ready?"

Walking into the living room to such a surprise turned her pale. Seeing the sight of your druggy friend's head barely attached to his body has that sort of effect. She's frozen in place; surely that crack high is gone now. The trail of urine from her crotch to the blood stained floor below was enough indication of being scared shitless. I won't kill her, but she will never forget this moment.

She's so scared she can't even scream. I walk over and I give her a warm embrace, smelling the similarly aged woman's own personal concoction of body odor, crack residue, and other fresh disgust.

As I hug her tight, I whisper in her ear, "You won't need these anymore."

Once her scapula disconnected from the socket, ripping the rest of her arms off was a breeze. Hearing the blood-curdling scream was orgasmic to me. The louder she yelled in pain, the wider my smile got. No one was going to hear anything. It was beautiful. Once she calmed down a bit, I patched her wounds with that good ol' Satan magic and I advise her to get the fuck out.

The armless woman stumbles out. I save her arms as souvenirs.

Now, what to do with this nearly headless crackhead wasting space in my living room? I make a beeline toward the open door in my room. The closet near my door glows warm red. Seems like the perfect place to hide a body and a couple of limbs. Shoving the woman's arms into the deep pockets of the dead crackhead, I drag the carcass easily. Don't know if it's because of his thin, wasted body or if I'm stronger now. As I place the body next to the door in my room, the rotary phone in the living room starts to ring. It's either Momma Smith's girlfriend Sister Margaret or Pastor Jackson.

The phone lacks an answering machine so most of the time ringing lasts a couple of minutes. I knew I had enough time to dispose of the bodies.

Opening the closet door reveals an abyss. Hundreds, thousands, and then millions of doors stretched along the wall of a mountain leading to an ocean of nothingness bordered by a canyon that stretched to infinity.

Times. Dimensions. Years. Eras. Races. Genders.

All representing those who had gone through my transformative process. Every face I gazed upon had a tale of surrender and revenge. Some were dropping off bodies as well. I pondered the ultimate realization of my fate. I realized I wasn't the only one.

Picking up the dead crackhead and watching his body fall hundreds of feet into the abyss, almost in slow motion, was quite the sight. Hitting the jet-black liquid, his body floats before something finally snatches it into the unknown.

"Oh shit," I say out loud.

That done, I pick up the still-ringing phone to hear the voice of a man who always managed to get under my skin. For a while I thought he was Satan's personal representative. Yup, Pastor Jackson of Mount Ebal Baptist Church.

"Well, hello son," he says in his smarmy voice. "Why don't you stop by the church so we can talk? And Sister Smith left something over here from the last time she was here." I told him I'd be over in about an hour.

Hopping into the shower, peculiar things started happening to my body. My epidermis felt like snakeskin and things went way strange when I started brushing my teeth. Spitting the residue of my 99 Cent Store toothpaste revealed a mixture of fluoride and blood. Glancing into the mirror, I can see my tongue almost split into two. My voice took on a deeper timbre and my eyes gave off a reddish hue. Hrm. Turning into a monster wasn't so bad. My abs looked amazing.

It had been a little while since the laundry was done but thankfully some drawers, an undershirt, t-shirt and shorts were available. Putting on lotion felt weird with the new developments, but I knew it was all part of the deal I made.

Founded as the city's first Baptist church, Mount Ebal served as the black cultural hub for more than 110 years. The church was named after one of the highest mountains in the West Bank. Some Bible chapter has this weird story about it being a cursed place according to Moses, then something happens and it transforms into a sacred place. Made sense to me because the land that Pastor Lee purchased for the church so many decades ago was once the scene of a massacre involving bootleggers and local authorities. No one wanted to buy the land as it was allegedly haunted. The owner then tried to create a local juke joint. Following some unexplained murders, the former bootlegger-turned-owner just disappeared.

The land sat for a while until Pastor Samuel Lee came to town. Using fifty dollars he had saved from his life as a sharecropper in Clarksville, Tennessee, Pastor Samuel Lee bought the land and founded Mount Ebal. He never worried about demons and ghosts. God was on his side.

For the people, the week's troubles were eased after a Sunday service. It was a spiritual drug; a moment in time that provided peace from the racially segregated nonsense that included housing discrimination, job discrimination, and even back then, police brutality. A backbone for the blacks living there, Pastor Lee created a safe place for community organizing and transformation.

Within the first year, Pastor Lee and several church auxiliaries ranging from the Mother's Board to Usher Board saved up roughly $350, which was a boatload of money back then. That allowed them to buy several acres of land, which later became known as William Edward Burghardt Park.

Pastor Lee preached and lived until he was 80 and a deacon named Augustus Jackson succeeded him. Growing up within the church walls, Augustus was a graduate of Southern University's class of '64 in Business Management. Becoming such a man of prestige, he found himself the first black man at some downtown accounting firm that no longer exists. Augustus had two children with his college sweetheart: Mae Rae and Paul. Living in suburbia had to be interesting, considering the Jacksons were the first black family to move in to the nearby suburbs on the city's Northside.

But the Jackson household was a strict one. It's the reason why Mae Rae left the household for Hollywood, becoming one of the most iconic models and R&B singers of the era. Meanwhile, Paul dedicated his life to the church and community. Graduating summa cum laude from Moody Bible Institute wasn't difficult for Paul, who also got a taste for political power through his start in student government.

After graduation, he rose through the ranks to become the right-hand man for the mayor. This came with perks for him personally but at the cost of a community he knew very little about and cared even less about.

When the mayor took pay-offs to bring in major corporate stores, Paul managed to convince us it was good for everyone as local favorites like Tim's Hardware and Mamma J's Theater closed down. He even did a good job convincing his father and the church that everything was for the better. Add the late 80s infiltration of that ready rock and he become one of those responsible for the cesspool our community had degraded into: something deformed and sick. When he retired from his job of wrecking the community from the top down, Paul took over Augustus's position at Mount Ebal as pastor. Membership grew astronomically. Hardships and inequality brought it on, I guess.

Even William Edward Burghardt Park became an open market for drugs, prostitution, and other illegal activities. There's an average of three or four deaths a month at that park. I had to destroy symptoms of their own oppression brought on by the good ol' Pastor Jackson himself.

Pastor Jackson hated me, but not as much as he hated my father. When Patcher Sr. wrote a newspaper article damning him for his ties to a corruption case around the then-mayor, things really weren't ever the same. But considering the weight our family once held in the community, things were kept civil.

Losing his faith, my dad ended up leaving the church completely. However, Mother suggested I attend with Granny as a way for me to learn a moral barometer and keep me out of trouble. I guess both my mom and dad didn't want me to be around them much since they were becoming targets of something much bigger than me. Me attending nearly every Sunday reminded my father of the man who attempted to ruin his reputation and drove a quarter of Mount Ebal's membership away.

The local Metro bus stopped right in front of Mount Ebal. Figured that was the better thing to do than walking. The church looked like I remembered. Stained glass windows featuring white Jesus, a large double door placed in the middle, and an old classic design dusted with all-white paint. There were some modern touches. The front marquee was replaced with a large LCD screen that slid between portraits of Pastor Jackson, a "helpful" word of the day, church service times, and social media handles. Underneath that was a third-party ATM machine and two vending machines: one with carbonated drinks and the other sold sweet and salty snacks.

Considering it was mid-day Saturday, Mount Ebal was somewhat empty. Looking into the large parking lot, there were only a handful of cars resting neatly within their stalls. The fully loaded Cadillac CTS meant Pastor Jackson was in his office. His secretary, known to the congregation as Nene, had her Lexus parked next to his. The rest of the cars must have been the few choir members who owned cars as everyone either walked or took public transportation.

Walking into the lobby, I can hear the choir practicing their A and B selections for the next day. They sound as soulful and funky as ever. While the world refuses to acknowledge their talents, the hood definitely understands their musical value. As I enter the church, they rehearse their vocal octave elevations of "Jesus Is on the Main Line." The tiny window into the sanctuary reveals how passionate they are.

Across from the larger double doors into the sanctuary was a smaller door that leads into a hallway. Passing the church kitchen, dining area, and Sunday school room, I found myself facing the office door for Pastor Jackson. On the his door were the words, "Jesus loves you".

Pressing the intercome button gently with my index finger, a sharp, yet familiar buzz lets off. Nothing happened. But I heard a rhythm of pounding that stopped after several time measures.

Finally, a muffled voice says with a level of exhaustion, "This is Pastor Jackson's office. How can I help you?"

I reply, "This is me, Patcher Smith, ma'am." Another buzz is heard and a lock releases the doorknob.

Opening the large slab of wood, chiseled to artistic perfection, revealed a room fit for a king. More so like a grand episode of MTV Cribs that I watched over at Uncle Ronald's house years back. Pastor Jackson's study painted a good picture of his history. Trophies, certificates, and medals all adorned the walls, celebrating his past victories. Wood floors, wood walls, wood desk. The finest oak, obviously. Nearby the door was a humongous 90-inch television set with ESPN playing sports highlights.

On the door's other side sat a small desk with one office chair occupied by Nene. Nene was a rosy mahogany cheeked, middle-aged woman with red hair wearing very late season knock-off Chanel. Some call her mad hood bougie. Known as Sister Nene Thompson by church members, she represented the congregation's desperate, mainly single female demographic. As married families took higher roles within the church social hierarchies, men were rare outside of deacons, ministers, and associate pastors.

She was a former pharmaceutical company executive secretary who found herself caught in a controversy involving her having sexual relations with her boss. Of course, once the wife found out about their ten-year-long affair, she threatened to take half. Hell hath no fury like a white women scorned, right?

As expected, Nene was let go, lost her pension, and any cash given to her by her boss was court ordered back to his wife. Moving back home, she found Christ and employment in the local post office. Pastor Jackson's charm was almost vampiric. Time had made her unattractive and he provided exactly what she wanted. Attention from a man of power. Even if it was borrowed.

I can tell she was exhausted from Pastor Jackson's strokes. The way she sat was awkward until she greeted me.

"Well, hello Brother Smith. How are you?"

"I'm alive, good enough," I reply.

"My condolences for Sister Smith," Nene says. "We're praying for you."

Pastor Jackson looks my way and says, "Blessed to see you, Brother Smith." He walks over and grabs my arm for a handshake. Well, he attempts. I have those demonic powers and all.

"Strong grip you have there, son," Pastor Jackson says.

"I've been working out a little."

"Sister Thompson, can you please leave us alone so we can speak?" commands Pastor Jackson. She obliges and locks the door at my mental command. Unbeknownst to him, his fate is sealed.

He walks back behind his desk that's covered with paperwork and a new iMac, among other office trinkets. Above his head is a large steel cross that hangs suspended by metal chains connected to anchors drilled in to the wall. It was gorgeous.

I get comfortable in the vintage wood chair but the tension becomes palpable. "You know Sister Smith was such a sweet soul and extremely active member of Mount Ebal Baptist Church," Pastor Jackson does his best job of giving calm before his storm. "Every Sunday, rain or shine, I could count on her to be sitting in the front row giving her all to the Father." Without missing a beat, he continues, "She was also a generous giver."

You got to be kidding me! I'm totally annoyed at the moment. "Cut to the chase, Pastor Jackson," I throw at him.

Pastor Jackson starts to stutter as he plays his next card of deceit. "Well, son, funds for the church have been low and so I've been digging into my…" he says before I cut him off.

"Your retirement, I presume," comes out in reaction. "Those lawsuits and settlements came back to haunt you, right?"

He avoids my comment and continues. "I know about your $200,000 inheritance and that could be enough to get us out," explains Pastor Jackson as he finally reveals his true intentions.

"But nigga, you just bought a CTS." My voice rises as I find myself angry at him and myself. Not only was he attempting to take advantage of my situation, I totally sold my soul to Satan when holding out several days could have changed my future.

Leaning back in his fuchsia Italian suit tailored to perfection, he says, "That was a blessing from God." My mind racing faster than a box Chevy fitted with a 454 block, I give up and realize that my fate is sealed and there's no turning back. Before my time to jump into the abyss myself, I might as well raise as much hell as possible. Make those who've wronged me and mine suffer. Now it's time for one of God's own. Pastor Paul Jackson.

A force beyond me pins him to the wall as I feel my voice getting deeper through every furious breath taken. My mouth feels lava hot. The chains holding the hanging cross began to loose slowly by just my thoughts. Pastor Jackson's study feels like something else wrapped beyond time and space itself. I let him have it.

"Blessing from God? Is a blessing from God watching you ride around in a luxury vehicle while the rest of your members, including my grandmother, struggle to ride the bus?" I demand. "A blessing from God is watching you pimp and shame helpless single women who financially hold up the church? A blessing from God is you spending years convincing Quesha to top you off when she was younger for you to just cast her off later? Guess that's why she sought a father figure elsewhere and had all those kids. She dropped out of high school and is using her experience with you on Johnny D at HD Chicken," I glare hard at him. "But why should you care? Your wife and kids live a happy little Christian life with your little home in the West Loop."

He has no time to reply as the chains loosen and the cross falls and sharply slices into the top of Pastor Jackson's skull at an angle. He's frozen as the part of his brain controlling breathing and muscle movement have been severed. Blood seeps from the clean cut, ears, eyes and mouth. Joining the life liquid flight, brain fluid took the train as well. A piece of his skull fell into his lap resting gently near his platinum ring. It's a struggle for him to even look at me.

Blessing? Yeah, I've given the hood and church a blessing. This time, from the earthly Leviathan; Lord of the Underworld.

Pastor Jackson's suit changes color as blood flows on the fine fabric. He's not dead yet; I can tell his heart hasn't stopped beating yet. It will, when the time is right.

But I won't be there to see because it's time to get that check. Getting to the money, right?

Chapter Three

Sundays after church were the busiest times at HD Chicken. But seriously, fuck the stereotypes; the joint offered some of the best fried chicken in the city, probably the state. Lines formed around the block with serving times sometimes nearing an hour for the golden brown poultry with a very distinct crunch. HD Chicken had been around longer than I'd probably been alive. Their menu was fairly simple and the actual building looked like a shack. I think it was owned by a Chinese family who didn't even care much about its customers. Hell, I doubt they even ate the food that probably killed as many people as the gangs and police combined. Then again, what does slow destructive nutritional value have against a Yelp score? Working the cash register every Sunday felt like preparation for the real hell. Except time moved at the speed of light and temperatures weren't as hot, but close enough.

That's what made Saturday nights so essential in terms of preparation. Chicken had to be properly seasoned with the packaged flour/seasoning mixture that featured more cancer causing chemicals than natural ingredients, biscuits composed of the same material as the rubber wedged between my socks and floor needed to rise, genetically modified vegetables that never rot had to thaw, and the diabetes-inducing apple pies had to be arranged from their boxes.

Getting there late meant HD Chicken had been closed for nearly an hour and the front door was locked. Since I was fired, the code giving access to the rear had probably been deactivated. Therefore, waiting for someone to see me out front was the key. The only people there had to be Johnny D, Assistant Manager Quesha, and prep-boy Anthony. A bushy beard and a wild afro made Anthony physically stand out but he was someone fairly common in today's age—someone who settled with a life of minimum wage and certain mediocrity. It's the only reason he felt compelled to finish prep by himself and mop the floors while Johnny D and Quesha fooled around. I figured the slob-of-a-manager was probably in the back office.

Anthony was a good guy enjoying the benefits of having both parents with very free spirits. He opened the door quickly. "What's good, mane?" he says enthusiastically. "I heard what happened yesterday. Daaaammn, nigga!" He chuckles before informing me Johnny D was in the back with Quesha.

Walking past the cash register, deep fryer, warming lamps, industrial oven, and sink lead me to the hall where Johnny D's office was located. Getting closer to the cheap plastic screen door, I hear that Johnny D and Quesha are occupied. My vision heightens. The wall disappears like a two-way mirror.

"Damn, baby, nobody gives brain like you," Johnny D slowly pants out.

"Hmmmm mmmmmmmm," is the only reply from Quesha's stuffed mouth. The beat of slurps and moans intensifies before Johnny D lets off a disturbing sign of ejaculation.

"So now, what about my raise?" asks Quesha. "My youngest son's birthday is coming up and you know his daddy don't do shit for him. I need the money."

This was getting good. Fairly entertaining. Like one of those Love and Hip Hop episodes I saw mindless teenage girls watching on YouTube during computer class.

"I've thought about your raise and unfortunately it's just not in the budget," says Johnny D without a fuck given. "Ever thought about selling your food stamps? Nice little side hustle."

I can see the tears welling in Quesha's eyes as she whimpered in confusion. "After all I've done? What about my son?"

The fat fuck responds while sipping old coffee from a porcelain mug that looked as if it hadn't been washed in days, "See, that's your problem. Should have gotten rid of it when you had the chance."

"Fuck you, nigga!" she spits out with anger.

Johnny D wasn't phased, not one bit. In fact, he felt empowered with his abilities to con people into his games. Digging his emotional knife deep into Quesha's heart, he joked, "Did that last Wednesday night and Thursday morning. Remember? Now see your way to finish cleaning the kitchen so we can both get the fuck outta here," says a dismissive Johnny D.

I feel a gust of wind as Quesha opens the door with force. Her tears make it down her company-issued blouse. She stops when she discovers my presence. I look at her with pity and understanding before she heads to the closet for the cleaning supplies. I'm disgusted for her.

Quesha was only a couple of years older than me. Her life was as bad as that movie where the fat chick from "The Parkers" kept yelling "Precious!" Forced into early adulthood, Quesha's mother was a few years younger. Folks around the town called her Lady T; she was model student before falling for the on and off again D-Boy at one trip to the library. She was there looking for a book relating to the lunar landing. Quesha's soon-to-be father Tawnto needed help with his upcoming GED, fumbling through the card catalog drawer.

One missed period later, she thought he was the one after he became her first. They loved each other to the moon and back. Quesha's mother changed him for the better. He changed her as well. Lady T's middle class upbringing involved a local community organizer who taught her the cause and effect issues that hurt the poor. She understood that more than ever and fought for better in him. Of course her parents publicly distanced themselves from her once the news came. She ran to Tawnto, who, on that day, decided against his past lifestyle.

There's a reality, quitting the drug game isn't like screaming fuck you, then happily living in the confines of a minimum wage job. In fact, Tawnto probably wished it was that easy. He still had to work and needed to sell out quick. As the pregnancy progressed, food, shelter, and prenatal care proved difficult with a cashier's job at Farmer's Groceries. What was more embarrassing, going from making five thousand a night to less than one hundred for bagging groceries or watching former drug associates whisper his lameness under their breath? The pregnancy attitude of Lady T didn't make things easier. Tawnto felt less of a man attempting to do the right thing. His schedule transitioned between work and studying for his GED. Life may not improve tremendously, but it'd be a lot better than now. He earned his GED midway through Lady T's pregnancy

But by the time her water broke, he had already eased his way back into the game and even had to drop a few niggas. Those bodies came back to haunt him once a young detective by the name of Ethan Bryant cracked those same killings. He realized Tawnto was a good shot. All the victims had gaping holes in their heads from hollow point bullets.

Her father was locked up for murder the day she was born. He'd just turned 18 years old that day. Ironically, he was planning on quitting the drug game again that day for a 9-to-5 at HD Chicken, after promising a few bottle tops of crack. That's when I realized there was a possibility of a fat crackhead—but I digress.

The baby would be named Quesha, after Tawnto's sister. Lady T gave birth to Quesha alone.

She got transitional housing and a small job at a refinery as a fire-watcher. It didn't pay much, but the job kept a roof over their heads. The problem was the long hours. This meant many nights, Quesha stayed with Tawnto's mother. The combination of an incarcerated father and workaholic mother didn't stop her from eventually engaging in the cycle of young pregnancy herself. That's not my problem though. Or maybe it is.

"I'm here for my check sir," I say as I open the door.

My goal: getting my money and leaving. To think of it, I don't even know why I was led here. Wasn't like I'm going to need it eventually. Maybe fate was giving me the power to fuck with him in a vile way. He just stares as I inch closer to his cheap laminated desk and he passes me the check inside an envelope.

Opening the envelope and lifting the flap of the paystub, I notice that my overtime was cut. "This isn't what I'm owed," I say gently. "The fuck man, all that overtime I did?"

He smacks his lips. Yup, he's also downing some food courtesy of HD Chicken. He has some hour-old chicken, mashed potatoes, gravy, nearly a day-old biscuit and corn that's been rolling around in butter for days probably. And is that a box cake that hadn't been properly thawed? Johnny D pauses for a moment, forms a wide grin and says, "Seems like you forgot to clock in those days, therefore, I don't owe you shit. Now get the fuck out my office, nigga."

This muthafucka. My scales get harder and I feel them spreading to other parts of my body. My neck even feels them. I feel my lungs take in more air than usual. My voice gets slightly deeper. "Nigga, if you don't give me what the fuck you owe me…" I growl.

"Or do what nigga," he retorts with confidence that doesn't realize its dead end.

I pause and decide to take a different approach. "That's a nice meal you have there. Quite a shame this is going to be your last meal."

"Fuck you mean?"

While he was still reveling in ecstasy from Quesha, I'd used my mind and possessed her to pour rat poison in his coffee. HD Chicken just so happened to have the non-flavor ones that kill rats upon notice. The little critters can tell what the cheap stuff is and they don't even bother. But for this rat, his short lifespan won't matter. I stand up taller and grin.

I see him starting to sweat, even more than usual for the fat bastard. This is going to be entertaining.

The zinc phosphide from the rat poison causes severe nerve damage. Watching him Harlem shake in his chair was enjoyable. For ten minutes, he rattled around grasping for life and hoping it would come. "What the fuck have you done?" Johnny D says in fragments.

"Ah, the rat poison is kicking in," I grinned.

I can see his stomach swell even larger than its natural state. Then the hemorrhaging starts. Not going to lie, watching this gross fat fuck get what he deserves is the crescendo to tonight's ordeal concluding with his cardiac arrest.

"Goodbye," I say sweetly.

Making my way out, I hear screams. Sounds like Quesha has discovered him.

Back at home, using the cheap Windows XP netbook at my disposal, I recite today's notes into the voice recorder and upload them to my almost bare SoundCloud account. I am satisified with the day.

I fall asleep to the dialogue for "Booty Call 2: But You Can't Use My Phone," courtesy of my unemployed and drunk neighbors.

Tomorrow is going to be a long day, I have to rest well.

Chapter Four

Sundays meant the banks were closed until the next day. I didn't have one of those fancy banks that allowed check deposits at their ATMs or even more modern, just snapping a pic of it with my phone. I was at a credit union Granny suggested. It was far from my place, but then again, I didn't need that shit anyway.

Where I was going, currency meant nothing. A day left until my homecoming. One more solid day of raising hell. After watching Johnny D succumb to his own nutritional and sexual gluttony, I replayed the previous night like the glory days of a high school football player scoring the winning touchdown and waking up to realize his mastery now was of the custodial arts.

I indulged in sleeping in for a bit—only a few hours though. The day was ripe for painting the town red. For such a beautiful nightmare that my reality had become, my dreams were happy.

Normally, I'd wake up around five o'clock in the morning, take care of Granny, shit, shower, and ensure decent oral hygiene. Granny was dead and I took a shit before sleeping. That meant hitting the shower and brushing my teeth. Time for breakfast.

Before the cancer hit, there wasn't a greater joy than cooking alongside Granny. I always called her the Julia Child of the hood. I, on the other hand, had the modern flair of Susan

41

Feniger. Always complementary, the joy of creating countless recipes from Red Velvet Cake to Beef Stroganoff led to the delicious moments of consumption. Life's joy was through a pot and wooden spoon. Who needs a fancy five star restaurant that I'd never be able to pay for. I could do it myself. But the hospice thing sort of killed that joy.

Our kitchen wasn't the best, but what are tools without the skillset? Like a photographer using a high-end camera and lacking knowledge of an f-stop? Pots, pans, and seasonings were available. I let fate decide my feast as papers from Granny's various cookbooks floated around the kitchen. And great taste they had. For this morning's breakfast: grits, eggs, pancakes, and salmon croquettes.

A box of Albers sat in the pantry alongside some flour, Aunt Jemima pancake mix, maple syrup, canola oil, and canned salmon. There were four eggs in the refrigerator, some onions, butter. A drawer nearby had the measurement tools required including spoons and a Pyre measuring cup. Finally, salt, pepper, garlic powder, and Lawry's Seasoning. For this, I'd also need two cast iron skillets, a griddle, and a small pot for the grits.

I started by turning on the back stove plate for the small, black nonstick pot. In front of that was one skillet with canola oil filling it halfway. This way I could get to the grits when I'm ready as that and the eggs would cook last. Indication of its heat came from small water bubbles dancing to the top before popping.

I chopped half an onion and drained the can of salmon. Blended those together with flour, egg, and a few seasonings.

After forming the mixture into three or four hand-sized patties, I could let each fry a few minutes before mixing the pancake batter and finishing off with the eggs. Every dish finished at the right time. For the first time in a long time, it smelled like days of past peace.

The remainder of a half-gallon of Tampico orange juice sat in the refrigerator. I sat that next to a red plastic cup, made my plate, and enjoyed the meal. My tastebuds felt as if they were gaining control over the metallic taste from days earlier. Feeling as if I was hyper aware of every protein, herb, and molecule on my plate. Plus, the presentation alone would make the likes of Pat Neely jealous.

For something that took nearly an hour and some change to fully prepare, it took only ten minutes to down. Before I finish the last bites of my feast and take the final swallow of my orange juice, I hear a loud pounding on the door in triplets at four seconds apart.

I finish the last of my meal without a care in the world. Whoever it is could wait. Being as I was only in my boxers, I make my way to a drawer in my bedroom. I sniffed a shirt and sweats before donning my garments so to not annoy the unknown guest with any unwanted aromas.

The triplet pounding on the door continues. Again, four seconds apart. Making my way toward the door, I open it.

"Well good morning, detectives. How can I help you today?" I greeted. I could tell from their stances that they're no strangers to these parts, considering the amount of weekly shootings.

The square-jawed Caucasian male asks for my name. I tell him. I notice a bald caramel colored man behind him. Nigga looked just as sweet as well.

"Mr. Smith, I'm Detective Roger Lowe and this is my partner Detective Ethan Bryant," he says. "A couple of homicides have been reported and we just wanted to ask you some questions."

I invite them inside. "Coffee, water, juice?" I asked.

"No thank you," both respond in unison.

Lowe and Bryant shuffle along to the same oak table I just ate breakfast on. That thing was sturdy than a muthafucka; it had been in our family for generations. We cherished the table like high priced diamonds. I guess the saying "those without much cherish the least" couldn't be more correct.

An awkward silence approaches like some shit is about to go down. They were going to ask me some investigative questions and I'd play around with the truth. Didn't make much sense to lie. Plus, in a minute's time, I had both of them figured out. This was going to be fun.

"Your Granny was always kind in leading us toward justice," said Lowe in a baritone that was Billy D like in every way. Guess he figured I'd walk in my Granny's footsteps. "Where were you yesterday morning and afternoon? Matter of fact, just give me a breakdown of your day," continues Lowe in his fairly basic questioning.

Giving him a breakdown of yesterday's adventure was easy enough. "Yesterday? Ah yesterday. I actually went and saw Pastor Jackson at Mount Ebal. Was quite an eye-opening meeting.

Then, I got my last check from HD Chicken and went home," I explained, feeling pleased about my articulation.

"What was your conversation like with Paster Jackson?" Lowe shoots back.

"My Grandmother passed a few days ago so Pastor Jackson gave me a few words of encouragement."

"Well, those may well have been his last words. But there wasn't any DNA or fingerprints at the murder scene," says Lowe before the set up. "Do you know if anyone would have a grudge against Mr. Jackson?"

"Good question, Officer," I play along. "Wouldn't have the slightest idea, I stopped going to church years ago once Granny got sick."

Now Detective Lowe got a lot more personal than I'd imagine when he asked why I quit going.

"Didn't see much of a point really." I sat back in my chair. "So are you going to arrest me?"

Both look puzzled. I can see their arms move closer from their knees to the hips of each respective gun holster at the top of their expensive cotton slacks.

"The fuck do you mean?" Bryant backs his superior.

"Alright, alright, I killed them both." The confession was hilarious. Wasting their time and then murdering them just sounded sweet in my mind. "But that doesn't mean you're going to arrest me and make it out of this apartment alive."

Detectives Bryant and Lowe rise with the quickness as both draw their guns. "Call for backup," demands Lowe.

"Copy. We're at Earl Long housing projects. Do you copy?" says a fearful Bryant. "Copy, we're at Earl Long… What the fuck? It's busted."

"Let me try mine," says Lowe before he realizes his was disabled through my magic as well. I can't believe I even gave him the time to check his signal-less iPhone.

"How about you both sit down and put your guns on the table?" I say without much authority in my voice, but they do it anyway.

The tables had turned. Well, to be true, it was never in their favor in the first place. Now fucking with them was pure enjoyment. They yell for help but no one hears them.

"Now I'm going to ask you some questions, but let's start simple," I say jovially. "How long have you been partners?"

"Help, Jesus please, God, somebody," is heard between both of them. It was only cliché to explain that the heavenly Father wasn't helping them today.

"Oh, just stop now. God can't save you," I said with glee. "So let's start this one mo geen': how long have you guys been partners?"

They both plead for help and commence screams. Their pupils fully focus and their hair raises. I can see small patches of sweat on their fresh pressed shirts. They were in some shit and they knew it. I ask them one last time.

"Third times a charm! How long have you been partners?"

"Fourteen years," Bryant screams in desperation.

"Good job, y'all," I give a congratulatory clap as I transition into question number two. "What's the average salary of a homicide detective round these parts?"

"Excuse me?" Lowe blends together words in panic.

If they're not going to answer, I'm going to kick it up a notch. Bryant and Lowe struggle as they are forced slowly to reach for their guns. Lowe stops a little early in his arm extension and ceases movement right above Bryant's testicles. Yup, pointed straight at his dick. Bryant raises his high enough for the barrel's end to kiss Lowe's temple. For added effect, I make them both squeeze the trigger just enough for the hammer not to engage the back of the bullet.

"Awwww yeah," I laugh.

"Alright! Sixty grand a year, give or take," he responds as a wet spot appears on his crotch.

No more games. Getting serious in five, four, three, two, one...

"How long have you been taking hush money from BGD and Westside Lords?"

"How do you know about tha..." comes from Bryant's mouth as I debate forcing Lowe to pull the trigger and then I make him pull it. Bryant screams but I mute him. I held his hand just high enough for his gun to still make out with Lowe's head.

"Hrm. Look at that shit," I remark. Lowe's screams complements Bryant's without the added pain.

"Alright! An extra 100K! Please let us go," Lowe cries out.

"What happened on May 5th, 2004?" I couldn't have sounded any more grand. They have blank stares. "You don't remember? How about I help you two a bit?"

Their eyes widen and I begin. "I was nine at the time. My father was a lead investigative reporter at The Tribune. I remember him telling me how crooked the police were, but I never paid it much mind. Figured doing the right thing meant the laws would leave you alone. But my father learned the hard way that wasn't the case as he attempted connecting corruption within the police department's ranks alongside local government. Somehow, my father was framed for distribution of several kilos of cocaine following a traffic stop. Now, there's no way a man who never smoked a cigarette, drank liquor, or spent time behind bars should get caught with drugs. That said, you two have to have known whose son I was and that's the reason you stopped by about all the murders."

A faint whimper is heard from Bryant's direction. He's losing blood fast as a puddle forms between his feet.

"How'd you know?" Lowe asked.

"You guys knew he washed his car every third Wednesday of the month," I said. "You bribed the local carwash guys to plant drugs in my father's old Honda. They found my father dead in his cell naked the next week with a knife in his chest and rupture in his rectum."

By then, Bryant had lost total consciousness. Didn't know if he was dead yet. No worry, I was going to kill him sooner or later.

"I'm sorry," Lowe says in a low voice.

"You will be," I retort. "Not only did you just now openly admit to orchestrating my father's set-up, there's a gun to your head and the gun in your hand just blew off Bryant's dick."

Now it was time for the question to top off the morning with these two fine officers.

"Who did you pay off to kill my mother?"

Singing like a canary, Lowe revealed the name of Luke Davis.

"What?" I asked. "You're talking about Hollow Point the rapper?"

"He lives in a mansion near South Barrington," Lowe screams as he gives the final detail.

I nod with satisfaction. "You orchestrated the murder of my parents and destroyed me—revenge would be killing you and digging your wife out. But if she's married to you, Mrs. Lowe is probably fucking around raw dog anyway. I'll spare the rest of your pathetic family further suffering."

Bryant's sitting corpse pulls the trigger. Blood, brain matter, and skull fragments spray paint the white refrigerator and cabinets. It was a clean enough shot to leave a gaping horizontal hole through his head. I can even see the base of his spine where parts of his brain once sat. Splitting flesh and bone, the bullet made him a distant memory.

There's a reason why I always viewed police and gang members as one in the same. Police spend hours within the day treating every citizen in our destitute environment as criminals. I remember Detective Lowe getting off for "accidentally" firing on a young girl during a drug raid of a wrong house.

Enjoying life with his wife and kids in a gated community thirty minutes away removed him from the reality of his damage. Those not picked off by law enforcement have to worry about other niggas as well. Gang members treat the streets like a large war zone without any formal rules of engagement. What are they fighting for? Property that doesn't even belong to them? Between the state sanctioned brutality from the police and institutionalized symptoms of gangs, they're both out to exterminate me. But I'll destroy them both.

And yeah, it's true, killing off some corrupt cops and gangbangers won't fix the problem. But it'll make me feel better at worst. At best, it'll scare the root of the problem.

I drag Bryant by his short curly head to the closet abyss. Lowe gets pulled from right under his chin. Knocking books, trinkets, other wasteful materials down along the way. They were rag dolls to me at this point.

After I dumped them, the table and fridge were wiped and I hit the mop. Wasn't the best cleanup job, but it'll do for now. Granny never taught me methods for cleaning human remains.

Now a shower. I use Granny's cocoa butter to hide the ash. Brushing teeth and putting on proper clothes were all that was left.

Today was the last day on earth. Who cared about laundry? For now, faded jean shorts and an old Miller Lite t-shirt was all that was necessary. To think, I'm going to have to kill the hood hero. The same man responsible for such local rap classics as "Fucken Yo' Favorite Bitch" and "10 Shots to tha 4Head" was also responsible for offing my own mother.

He'll be dealt with accordingly in due time. Right now, I'd like to see my Uncle Ronald. Best I apologize for the other night. The prepaid phone Granny used had a good ten minutes left before needing to add more. That's all I was going to need anyway. By the time I pick it up and start the dialing prompt, it's almost eerie how the phone rings and his name pops up on the small phone screen.

"Hey Uncle Ronald. How's life treating you?"

"I'm alright," Uncle Ronald responds. "You don't have to be so guarded. You're handling it a lot better than people double your age."

He invites me over since his wife is making tacos after she gets back from spin-class. Being the uncle he is, Ronald asked me to get him some Newports and some lottery tickets—more specifically, two quick pick straight boxes.

"Aye nigga, times is hard and this funeral expensive as fuck," he explains with a chuckle.

I don't mind much. Uncle Ronald was always the type of uncle who did what he could even with his limited amounts of resources. Plus, he had a needy, yet highly attractive wife and five kids. Three were his and the other two from Porcshe. They made a cute couple. He was the quiet assertive one while she was the more aggressive type. It worked for both of them. At this point, they were the only ones who probably gave an honest two shits about me. Guess this why I didn't mind doing this favor. Even my newly found demon abilities didn't tear away all of my heart. An inch of heart can sometimes get you farther than one thought, even if that would be solely dedicated to destroying the one man who murdered my mother. Esther Smith will be avenged.

"Alright, give me like 30 minutes to an hour," I said before good-byes were exchanged.

Chapter Five

Out the door and then right back in once realizing I didn't have much money. I didn't care much about my flimsy $70.80 check from that shitty part-time job but the only cash in the slim mold of my nearly empty wallet was five bucks. Shuffling quickly to Granny's stash underneath the bed could net me a few more bucks. I laid out flat on the floor and the box was near the center of the bed. Meaning you had to work a little harder and be just lanky enough. Thankfully, the crackheads from a few nights ago didn't find it. It was a vintage Stacy Adams box that looked its thirty-plus years of age from the wear and tear. I pull it close to my chest while on all fours. Opening the lid revealed around 30 one-dollar bills. Some crinkled, some folded in half amongst the loose change.

As I'm about to grab a few bills, hands reach out from underneath the old wooden queen size bed and drag me underneath. Everything goes black. The jade-eyed woman from my dream appears in complete darkness, only illuminated by a deep red spotlight. Same hips, breasts, and skin.

"See you tonight," she whispered sensually.

Everything goes black again. I wake up harder than ancient calculus. Funny thing, my time is running out and all I can think about is that ass. What's become of me?

It wasn't too much of a hassle going to Huntington subdivision about ten miles southeast. Since I was also making a personal delivery, I took my trusty backpack filled with discarded gum wrappers, some change, my netbook, and its nearly broken charger. Before catching the 214 bus, I hit the gas station convenience store across the street. A neon-light marquee hung above the entrance flashing out Beaver Creek. A homeless man smelling like tomorrow's punishment and Thunderbird opened the door before standing back in his spot awaiting someone to spare him some change.

Making my way to the cooler, I reach and get a cheap Arizona Iced Tea, head down the candy aisle for some Red-Hots and grab a bag of Hot Fries on the way to the line. Standing in line is a Latino man, fairly tall and muscular, who is adding minutes to his pre-paid card. From the wife-beater, trainers, and sweats, he looks like he just left the gym. Sandwiched between he and I is a middle aged white woman with a long trench coach and Ray-Ban shades. As tall as the lady's abdomen is a large Golden Retriever. He doesn't like me very much by the sound of that defensive bark.

"You calm down, Noah," she says as she turns around and smiles my way.

"Oh it's alright," I respond as she turns back and takes her turn at the register.

The dog turns around and barks madly again. In return, I contort my face in odd directions. I show some of my fangs for added measure. Noah cowers and proceeds to shut the fuck up. She purchases a pint of Malibu rum and a two-liter of Coke.

"That'll be $13.68," says the older black woman behind the register. Deep down, she hates her minimum wage living here. Regardless, she presses on. "Alright, honey that's a twenty right there. $6.32 is your change, ma'am," the casher belts in a loud but articulate voice.

"Oh. Wait. I need a $200 money or....."

"Everyone get the fuck down or get ya fucking top blown off!" shouts the armed gunman rushing into Beaver Creak with his partner in crime. Dumb criminals at best.

The ski masks didn't help their lack of shirts, as the tattoos were identifiable. The darker skinned one with dreads had the typical markings. The one under his abdomen read "Money Over Bitches." Another on his right pectoral muscle said "R.I.P. Louis J." An AR-15 with extended clip served to accentuate his purpose.

The other fairer skinned co-conspirator had shiny gold fronts and a tattoo of a child on his heart. Could be anyone. A sister? Daughter? The white ski mask he wore contrasted against his black Mossberg pump action shotgun.

But it doesn't matter; they're both going to be welcoming death's door soon. I got especially heated when they shot the blind lady's dog for the sake of shutting it up. Sure, the barking was annoying, but not enough to off man's best friend. Come on now!

Watching the blind lady and cashier fall to the ground was second nature for them. Focused on so much of everything else, I forgot to heed to their commands. The close range shotgun blasts passed me and hit the potato chips on their aisle.

Brushing off the crumbs and bits brought by the mix of Funyuns, Fritos, Takis, and other salty snacks took a second. I get up. Looking out through the convenience store window, I see the bus I normally take to Uncle Ronald's place simply pass by.

"Man, fuck this." I get back up with fire in my eyes and the underworldly bass in my voice.

BOW! The buckshot pellets fly past me as I run toward the light skinned nigga. He tries to shoot again but it jams. Stiff and scared, I loosen him up with one slight touch of his stomach. And just like that, he shatters into a million organic pieces. I almost felt like Doctor Manhattan in this muthafucka.

"The fuck?" the other gunman alive, for now, said.

He was so mind-fucked watching his homie get blown to smithereens that he forgot the reason he was there in the first place. The dumb ass just decides to unload his entire clip into me. It takes about a minute and I just stand there. His aim is good enough at least. More than half the bullets go through my left eye, throat, lungs, stomach, spine, and he even clips a few fingers and toes.

The damaged tissue repairs itself almost instantly. I step within an inch of him. He's terrified and drops the assault weapon. The cashier was too frightened to even look above the counter and the blind lady was, well, blind. Today, it's probably for the best.

I get him in a real good headlock with my weakest arm, the left. My right arm is for something even better. They both should be able to hear the sound of flesh ripping from the multiple layers of skin tissue, the nerves snapping, blood vessels exposed, muscles snap as the capsule departs from the cartilage.

Oh, the screaming involved! Man, that boy hollered as I detached his arm from his body.

Guess beating the rest of his life out of him with the same ripped arm couldn't have been more insulting.

Enough with this playing around. I still have to get to Uncle Ronald's crib so lunch doesn't get cold. Making my way to the door, I double back to the cash register.

"Hello, ma'am," I say while glancing over the counter. I can tell she's pale in the face, yet black as night. Doesn't help there's an ear from one of the dead thugs next to the timed change lock underneath the credit card receipt collection.

"Hello, ma'am." I say again. Maybe my calm deep voice will usher her out of the initial shock of what just happened. I am close enough to see her name tag reads Bertha.

"Excuse me, Bertha. Can you get me a box pack of Newport menthols and two quick pick Powerball tickets, please?"

She looks up horrified. Fingers, hands, and arms shake in fear as she reaches to the cigarette display.

"Oh yeah, here's my ID," I smile at her. "I just turned 18 some days ago."

"That won't be necessary, sir." She grabs a pack of Newports and places them in front of me. She starts the prompt on the Lotto machine. The two tickets come right after another. Must have been difficult to do the job with all the carnage that just took place. The cleanup is going to be monstrous.

Bertha quickly puts both on the counter and hits the floor again. I leave her alone.

"Well, all this and the drink and snacks as well, so I'll just leave this $15 here for you. Keep the change," I say as I grab a brown paper bag from the counter stack.

Skipping out of Beaver Creek gleefully, I sit on the bus stop bench, just watching the scene unfold around me. Soon enough, the cops and ambulances make it in. You can hear the "Oh, shit!" and "My God!" from across the street. This is something they weren't used to. A level of death unforeseen. Saying the authorities on the scene were disturbed was more than an understatement.

The blind lady cried as she realized her faithful dog was gone for good. That moment hit me hard. She lost something special to her by cowards with ill-gotten weaponry. The feeling was mutual.

Bertha was carried out on a stretcher and repeatedly screamed, "I saw pure evil today! It was the devil himself up in there!" They were taking her to the loony bin for sure.

A few minutes later, the gaggle of reporters and news vans show up. For them, it was a great news story: a simple attempted convenience store robbery turned into a bizarre double homicide. Miraculously, no security footage was found.

My cheap watch reveals the time to be at the tip of 1:30PM as the bus arrives. On the side was an advertisement for Hollow Point's recently released album *Shank*. It's got a popular tune that gets played a billion times a day on nearly every radio station. Hell, the teen in the seat across from me is already annoying me as he plays "Fucking They Favorite Bitch" on his smartphone.

For those looking for some insight into the incredibly deep lyricism, here's what the hook sounds like:

> *Death to niggazzzzz that snitch*
> *Cause I got figgazzzz and fucking they favorite bitch*
> *Fucking they favorite bitch*
> *Fucking they favorite bitch*

Obviously, hearing some young nigga on the bus reciting those God-awful bars is annoying, even at medium volume. I notice his rendition is making the few people riding this line uncomfortable. *Jeez, there are kids around. How rude.* Regardless, I attempt to ignore him while snacking on the chips and iced tea. He gets louder.

Finally, I give him a look after turning around to the opposite side of the aisle.

"We got a problem?" said the adolescent with knockoff Ralph Lauren Polo shirt and leather Jordan 9's. Those sneakers were probably fake, too. He looked as if I disturbed his daily dose of musical malnutrition. As he was pulling off his headphones, he gave a hard eye roll. A part of me wanted his eyes to freeze in position. Wouldn't pain me. And I could do it by just thinking about it, but I decide to try and reason with this young thug.

"You're at an eleven," I explain to the young one. "Mind turning that down to about a six?"

A blank stare meant he gave zero fucks. Disrespectful muthafucka he was.

"Fuck you talking to nigga?" spouts out as his nose flared. Add a tongue ring and tight skinny jeans, he could have been a closeted homo. Not my business though. I just want him to shut the fuck up. "Get the fuck out of my face with that bullshit, mane," he says before putting his Beats By Dre headphones back on.

Just to set me off, he cranks up the volume. The music keeps him in a trancelike state including rhythmic head nods. Reciting the lyrics indicates full immersion.

She swallowed all my cum like bubblegum
'Cause I got funds and her nigga got none

I see red literally. *The audacity of this lil' nigga.* I notice my off point was three bus stops away; up in the next couple of hundred feet. The fake ass Jordan wearin' nigga had one of those low-cost Android phones from an off brand cell phone provider. Shit, I'm surprised he had a good enough signal to even stream the *Shank* album.

I start in on him right after the stop on 5th and Coleman Boulevard. The volume reaches excruciating painful decibels. He quits the music application and restarts, but that fails to boot.

Maybe freeing his RAM will help. Twitter, Facebook, Tinder, and Leafly all shut down in quick secession.

"6th and Coleman," an electronic voice announces out of the bus speakers.

His phone's non-removable battery gets smokey. He tries to throw the phone but it's stuck to his hand. It sparks then catches on fire and then his hand is engulfed in flames.

Now I'm a few feet from my bus stop as the bus driver looks up in his rear view mirror.

The bus screeches to a halt as both front and rear doors fly open quicker than the hiss the air breaks make.

"Everyone get off the bus!" the tall, bald bus driver barks and everyone scrambles towards the exits.

"Somebody! Help me please! Help me!" These roaring loud screams of desperation have replaced his favorite club hit. Stop, drop, and roll becomes an elementary lie to him. The screams only worsen the situation. For each inhale he takes for the next scream, carbon monoxide finds a new spot in his lungs. Judging from the melting plastic on his feet, those sneaks were counterfeit. Fear sends fecal matter running down the side of his Girbaud jeans.

The bus driver breaks the glass case holding a fire extinguisher. Removing the release pin from the extinguisher, the fire retardant fails to spew from the short rubber hose.

"Oh, fuck this," the bus driver says before hopping off the bus and stepping clear.

Outside, one of the passengers dials 911 and requests assistance. Others pull out their phones and start recording and shooting photos. Spectators make Facebook posts and Tweets. A few even post selfies like the sociopathic creeps they are. There was even this one young female freestyling using the situation for a bar on Snapchat.

By then, the flames have covered the teen's body. Watching from outside the bus, he is charred beyond recognition. His skin reminded me of burned candle wax. The hypovolemia sets in as his fatty parts are roasted. Didn't take that long for the pain to cease as that underworld transition proceeds.

I got a right pivot to make on Uncle Ronald's street. Then a quarter mile walk. Not too far, almost there.

Chapter Six

Uncle Ronald was way closer to me in age than he was to his older brother, my father. In his mid-30s, he was a man with quite the charm. Though Dad and him had different fathers, their love for each other surpassed it, though it didn't stop their lives from going in vastly opposite directions.

Patcher Sr. found himself excelling academically and artistically at a very young age. Too bad that shit never rubbed off much on me. Getting a full-ride scholarship to Howard University was a cakewalk for his quick mind. Unfortunately, that same brilliance didn't foresee the eventual set-up from the powers that be. But I guess MLK and Malcolm didn't see it coming either. Or, maybe they did.

Part of his success came from having his father Moses around enough to keep him in check, offer guidance, and keep him looking fresh to impress. Even after the divorce of my grandparents, Patcher Sr. felt enough love to eventually become a productive citizen, marry my mother, and create the mess you know now.

Granny's next relationship a few years later turned a decent family situation into hell on earth. Patcher Sr. was with Grandad

Moses for the night when Granny Smith decided to hit the local nightclub for a night out with the girls. Since the divorce was due to infidelity, Granny Smith was over the idea of companionship.

Granny Smith and Grandpa Moses were each other's first. As time moved forward and Patcher Sr. became part of their lives, Grandpa Moses felt trapped. And there's a chance Granny Smith felt the same way as well. The end to their legal union felt amicable, though Grandpa Moses never quite found another woman like Granny Smith.

Granny Smith felt the same way apparently as she had just as much of a difficult time moving on. As she was the primary caretaker of Patcher Sr., bringing other men around Patcher Sr. every other week or month felt disrespectful to her. Instead, Granny Smith used her free time between the local soup kitchen where she worked and service to Mount Ebal as president of the homeless ministry to go out privately and enjoy male companionship.

On one late evening, the sounds of "(Not Just) Knee Deep" and "Don't Stop Till You Get Enough" blared through the nightclub as a disco ball cast its sparkling light over the partiers. The packed venue was full of people dancing away the tough day without a care for tomorrow. Body heat and sweat coming through dresses and polyester shirts meant a successful night. But the hyped crowd didn't impress Granny Smith much as she sat in the faux leather booth.

Advances from male suitors didn't impress her much either. They were too aggressive, too timid, or just corny. But then she met Uncle Ronald's father Joshua Johnson, known as JJ, and he seemed like the perfect man. Slim, perfect jawline, fashionable beyond belief, beautiful teeth, and quite the gentleman.

JJ approached her booth as "Fame" blares through the speakers. David Bowie never sounded so good at the moment for Granny Smith. He ignores her co-workers gabbing next to her, sits directly next to her, and whispers in her ear. "My name is Joshua, madam, but the folks round these parts call me JJ. Would you like something to drink?"

With a sly smile, Granny nods in agreement. In her mind, the future is already set. Another chance for marriage, kids, home and life with someone who appreciated her. All JJ needed was her name.

"You, sir, can call me Gladys." Six months later, constant vomiting found itself the final indicator of pregnancy alongside bits of light lactating.

Things were beautiful to start. JJ's work at the nearby tire plant gave them some sense of security. That's where his confidence came from.

But JJ's downfall came from the drinking and, in the meantime, hustling. Granny became the breadwinner and the humiliation from the neighborhood rapidly turned him into a monster. The heavy arguments graduated to beatings. Patcher Sr. and Uncle Ronald saw terror that normally breaks children. Every hook to Granny's jaw, foot to her face, and bruise on her body enraged both overwhelmingly defenseless children. Late nights indicated side-hoes who did everything they could to fulfill his fragile male ego.

Then one night, Uncle Ronald, who wasn't even two years old, watched as a drinking rant led to JJ blowing his own brains out with an old Smith & Wesson.

Thus Uncle Ronald's path was set. An angry black kid with a large chip on his shoulder. Madness always followed him. Watching Patcher Sr. getting more attention and wholesome parental love because his father was still alive drove Uncle Ronald into an envious rage at times. He was well aware of his emotional handicap from an early age. Father and Son days at school became rudimentary exercises of embarrassment. Father's Day became no different than the hours leading to. Having an active father gave Patcher Sr. foresight into potential obstacles, but Uncle Ronald just had to learn life's more important lessons in manhood on his own.

Ronald found power through street pharmaceutical sales for the Westside Lords. Granny kicked Uncle Ronald out of the home once she found him working his wrist over a stove. Going full-time on the streets meant dropping out of high school after his sophomore year.

Nothing scared him. That life has a way of making fear take a back seat. Paranoia and the pressures of this kind of employment leads to mental urban decay. *Trust no nigga, nor bitch.* In his eyes, everyone was the potential enemy. Death knocked on his door daily for a collection; Uncle Ronald just smiled and delivered a bold middle finger from his right hand, as he clutched his 9mm in the left.

For every brush with death or possible lifelong incarceration, he overindulged in the activities of a young hood prince. The clothes and expensive European sports cars made him feel like more of a man than his dead father ever was. VIP treatment at the club felt like validation. Honest minimum wage living was some chump shit. Casual sex became a part of the lifestyle. Hoes were plentiful enough and willing to do any and everything for a Birkin bag or Red Bottoms. He'd conquer women from far and wide.

"More hoes, than clothes," he'd say.

And the baby mommas followed. One after the other after yet another. Two boys and one girl. All in a two-year span. Watching a few associates get struck down with AIDS and herpes didn't deter him from a wild lifestyle. Cook more work and make more sales was the motivation for his daily game of Russian roulette. His kids were spoiled in every imaginable way possible. Nothing made him feel like more of a man than taking care of his own.

But that way of life also came with its fair share of enemies, something Uncle Ronald was very aware of. He was a known monster throughout the hood, but never an abomination as he stuck to a strict code of honor, which served him well in earning respect. While many gang members took a spray-and-pray approach to gunplay, Ronald practiced weekly at the gun range an hour away. When he shot, his bullets always hit their target with a SWAT team level of accuracy. Women and children were never to be hurt, but talking to the police was worse than death.

No one could change him. No one except a stripper named Exotic. Her friends called her Porsche. Ronald befriended her after seeing a patron of hers get out of control crazy. Making a man cum on himself during a lap dance sometimes means catching feelings that clearly aren't reciprocated in a monetary transaction. Uncle Ronald pistol-whipped him to an inch of his life once he heard her scream during the rape attempt. Then she shot him with her registered pistol discreetly placed in her knock-off Louis Vuitton purse.

Porsche had a few toddlers herself. That was enough for her anyway. Plus, the last abortion destroyed her uterus, preventing more offspring. From their perspective, they were officially over having children anyway. A few dates turned into a lasting commitment from one another. Porsche and Uncle Ronald were tired, something they were both honest enough to admit to one another. Thus, the early beginnings of the hood Brady Bunch. Who cared if she once had friendly pussy? Did it really matter that he had three baby mothers?

Uncle Ronald didn't even bother selling the rest of his work, he just gave it back to his plug. The club appearances were near marketing attempts as the clothes he wore were fake, the cars were leased, and the most expensive thing he actually owned was a safe at a stash house. Porsche went back to nursing school at nights while Uncle Ronald studied for his GED during the day. They collaborated and found themselves living much better. A day after earning his GED, a job was waiting for him at an offshore refinery. A month later, they made things official and tied the knot at a nearby justice of the peace.

Together, they made enough to live a decent life and the children got most everything they wanted. Their pasts mattered none. The future couldn't have become better. They weren't rich, but lived peacefully. And right now, it was a typical Sunday.

Uncle Ronald chilled in his garage listening to the radio, reading the sports section, and smoking the last Newport in his pack. There was enough room to chill in the two-car garage. But only Uncle Ronald's '96 Monte Carlo SS was there as Porsche was out for the afternoon. Guess I came right on time. He's just happy with the goods.

"Good looking on the smokes and quick picks, my nigga," says Uncle Ronald as we exchange urbanized handshakes.

I sense he's on edge about his mother. The small shakes in his war-torn hands as he removes the wrapping plastic around the cigarette box affirm my suspicion.

"How the funeral arrangements going?" I ask.

Uncle Ronald takes one cigarette, places it behind his right ear, and puts another between his ashy lips. He pulls a black Bic from his faded sweatpants pocket and he crouches forward a little as he lit the Newport for one long drag.

"Shit, nigga," he says, letting out a large puff of menthol. "Just figuring out how the fuck this is getting paid for. Your father's funeral nearly bankrupted us... if it wasn't for Granny's social security checks... And the mortuary wants 10 racks for everything."

Times were hard enough for Uncle Ronald to consider getting back into the life. Several years removed from the drug game, he knew a few calls to make just in case. Had to be a difficult battle between doing the right thing and being broke. Didn't help that the Post Office he now worked at was cutting jobs. The mediocre pleasure of overtime made the possibility of earning extra bread farfetched. He offered some words of encouragement and assistance anyway. "Look, I know you got your own personal hell and shit, but you got a place to stay until you get yourself together," assures Uncle Ronald. I was appreciative, but had to let him know the obvious without freaking him out.

"Making my exit sir, not going to the funeral," the volume lowered with every word.

"Fuck you mean, nigga?"

"Leaving tonight; plane ticket already bought," I answered.

He looks at me and stands up. I follow suit and we both exit the garage through the door leading into the living room. Uncle Ronald walks to the kitchen across the hall and grabs a couple of water bottles. I sit near a dining table topped by nearly expired coupons, an ashtray, plastic fruit, and weed crumbs. He tosses the bottle directly at my hand.

The kids were occupied with typical distractions in their rooms. "Violent Open World Shooter, Sequel 35" kept the boys busy. Meanwhile, girls transitioned between YouTube clips of the newest Rihanna video and looping Vine clips.

"You can't run from this shit you know," he says looking at me directly.

As I meet his gaze, Porsche walks through the front door holding groceries in one arm and a few gallons of water in the other. Uncle Ronald moves toward her to offer assistance.

"I got it, bae," he says.

"Thank you, hun." She smiles and kisses Uncle Ronald on his lips.

He gathers up the bags and then sets everything in hand on the countertop.

"You know, that damn Shonda forgot to give me back my EBT card," an annoyed Porsche says.

"Don't even worry about it wit' yo' fine self, guh," Uncle Ronald reassures as he grabs her waist and pulls her in for a kiss.

Porsche grabs a handful of his junk and whispers loud enough for me to hear, "Shit right here mine and don't you forget, nigga," as I try not to chuckle and fuck up the mood.

"Alright, alright, bae, chill out. We got company," he laughs.

"Hey Patcher! You good?" Porsche hollers across the room. "I know you hungry, nigga."

"I could eat," I reply to her. Then I lower my voice and look at Uncle Ronald who has settled back across from me at the table. "Yo Uncle Ronald, I know what happened to my mother and father."

"Oh shit! What?" he says as he grabs my arm. "Baby, me and Patcher gotta go outside for a minute."

We duck into the garage and he says, "How the fuck do you know? No. Wait." He takes another Newport out of his box, lights it and takes a long drag. He's shaking. I've never seen Uncle Ronald like this before. "There's a reason your father's murderers in jail were never found," is the first thing that comes out after he exhales. "Ya pops was working on a big blow-up story; he started with the police department and their connection to the local gangs. Matter of fact, that's one of the reasons why I got out the life."

Seeing my father sentenced to life in jail for conspiracy was an ironic way of silencing him. Word around town pointed toward lifers who killed Dad. Didn't make much sense to go after them, dying in prison was torture enough. Dad knew his fate, but didn't give a single fuck. There were moments where I resented him for that. The kid in me thought he didn't care about my well-being. Now though, I get it.

"To be true, I wanted to find every muthafucka involved and mail their body parts to any remaining family, but ya dad reminded me of my own family."

From my dad's position, I wouldn't be surprised if he knew Uncle Ronald didn't understand the level of sophistication those in power had. He asked exactly how I discovered everything.

"My newly found omnificence, plus an envelope full of letters from Dad last week," I replied.

Uncle Ronald didn't catch my comment about omnificence. That, or he just didn't know what it meant and didn't want to come off as ignorant. But he could tell I was planning on doing something stupid. He also knew he couldn't stop me.

He looked at me deeply as he took another drag from his Newport. One last plea came from my favorite unc's mouth, "You're a good kid, Patcher; you ain't gotta do this."

But we both knew that I did. South Barrington was a suburb way across town so dinner would be too time consuming to even stay for. I had some business to take care of now and that couldn't wait any longer.

"See you later, Uncle," I say and stand up.

"Be careful, my nigga," Uncle Ronald says before grabbing me for one last hug. But that moment reminded me of what little family I had left. I decide to wait a little, watch some TV with my favorite uncle and eat dinner with the family.

We had tacos that night. I even helped shred the vegetables. For a moment, I almost regretted my decision to be take on these powers. Maybe holding on a little longer would have made life brighter.

Maybe I'm just in my feelings at the moment. But I ain't got no time for those. Hell, I already killed the men responsible for my own personal misery: those who conspired against my father. Taking out the bastard responsible for my mother's murder will round things off nicely. Doesn't matter how fast, slow or elaborate Hollow Point's death will be.

I'll be doing anyone with working ears a favor by silencing him. Then again, if I kill Hollow Peezy, he'll just be immortalized by the hood as a legend regardless of how mediocre his music is. Thankfully, those fans will die off.

It just so happens that tonight is Hollow Point's annual Summertime Hoes, Drank & Dank celebration. I might not be the freshest dressed, but wait 'til they get a load of me. This will be a party to remember.

Chapter Seven

Sunday
8:00PM

"It's in the music and on the idiot box," one middle-aged fellow says to another on the seats across from me.

They must have worked as janitors or maybe employees at the nearby fertilizer plant. I could tell by the tattered jumpsuits and worn workbooks. Must have been a long, exhausting Sunday. The funk coming from both served as better proof. They wore name tags, one with James and another saying Rob. To be this old and struggling to get by has to be infuriating enough to hate the world sometimes. More so for a world they haven't seen much of. Their perspective was limited by a lack of opportunity for growth. Those in that position can only blame the alleged misdeeds of those at the top. Rumors and gossip become accepted truths allowing false weaknesses to artificially release them of their daily agony.

"Yeah man, I heard Jay Z, Oprah, Obama, and even that nigga Hollow Point were all members of that Illuminati shit," Rob said as he turned slightly to reveal "bert" on his name tag. I guess his name is Robert. "You know they have to do blood sacrifices and all that satanic shit just to get rich."

"They run the world, too," James says as Rob nods in agreement.

"I saw one video on YouTube that gave a real ass explanation of how Lady Gaga is the anti-Christ," Robert says before turning my way as if they had knew I'd been listening in.

"What you think, lil' nigga?" James says as he looks my way.

I paused for a second. "Well, they rich and we broke as fuck so there must be something to it." They both look disconcerted by my statement. The train announces the time as 8:30pm before the indication of my stop in the South Barrington. I stand up and make my way to the doors. "But you can't blame them if that's the route they want to take, to be honest," fires out of my mouth right after. I step off the conveyance.

I definitely meant that. Life is hell for many, why not join an exclusive organization that controls global citizens? Must be special if you're in the company of those members anyway. If I didn't already make my deal, joining a Satanic set full of wealthy artists, politicians, and moguls sounds like a life upgrade. Most folks work their entire lives at a job they hate for little to nothing in return. Who needs a soul when mansions and fly whips are so enticing? Funny how Satan is blamed for their success. If so, I figured they should be thanking evil.

Evil surely got Hollow Point to the top. The multiplatinum singles and albums, house in the suburbs and luxurious lifestyle made him my hood's success story. We all know the story: single parent crack baby creates music from his laptop in-between drug runs and assassinations. Even being on house arrest didn't stop him from reaching his dreams of escaping the madness surrounding him. Then, a local hit turns into a viral sensation. Hollow's first single from his debut mixtape "Coagulation" was fitting for someone who found themselves leaving murdered bodies in strange areas for days.

For someone from the hood who grew up with a *Trust no nigga* attitude, he threw himself at the mercy of the record label executives who signed him to a fairly lucrative deal. Some called him phony and a sell-out for leaving the hood once he got rich. But it made sense as he still had enemies in the streets who wanted him dead. Guess you can add me to the long line, but unlike the others, I'll get the job done.

Between having to watch his back in the streets and within the industry, one could tell that Hollow Point was growing into a life of self-destruction. Didn't matter since he was selling out shows in every city he went. The people loved him. By the time of his debut major release, "I'm a Murderer," he couldn't do a performance without a cosmic cocktail of lean, some blow, and Bacardi. But nightmares of the lives he took, both deserving and innocent, still kept him up at night before the doctor-prescribed Ambien kicked in.

For enemies and other rappers coming for his spot, he had hitters from the hood willing to do anything for a chance out themselves.

He'd even turned his ride-or-die chick GangBang into a global female icon herself. Hollow owed her that as she had accompanied him on several of his drive-bys. Not going to lie, her "Head 'Til I'm Dead" track is catchy as fuck.

Snippets about my mother flash back vividly as I keep walking to my goal. Father was already in jail and the feds never stopped finding ways to fuck with her. Growing up a product of the foster care system made her a tough cookie regardless. After aging out, she found work at the same soup kitchen my father's mother worked at. They became close enough for her to be the daughter she always wanted.

"Honey, I got someone you may want to meet," Granny said as she introduced her to my dad who was covering his first story as an intern for the Tribune. She didn't know they were already familiar. But this time, they were finally ready for each other. Mother continued to work at the soup kitchen and eventually moved on to a better paying position at a nearby homeless shelter.

Didn't matter if it was an administrative position, she always found ways to interact with the poor. She didn't mind my father ruffling feathers after their marriage and having me, as long as he did it for a just cause.

Eventually, she became disillusioned with the city government when my father dug deeper into a state corruption story that tied local drug trades to City Hall. I remember strange vans that followed her around as she did everyday errands such as going to the grocery store or dropping off and picking me up from school during the week.

The day it happened, the Mount Ebal morning choir had barely finished the first part of "Jesus is on the Main Line" ahead of the gunfire that sprayed the church and their main target, my mother in her Chrysler Sebring.

Bullet number one hit Tia through her right hip, traveling slightly higher as it severed her lower spine. Bullet two split her large intestines and exited by her lung making her collapse near the automatic shifter. The final shot to the right temple ended her. That didn't stop bullets number four, five, six, seven, and eight making her body look like bloody Swiss cheese mixed with raw ground meat. I was on the toilet taking a shit from a recent stop by HD Chicken; the gunshots sounded like Al Qaida had arrived in the front parking lot. Thankfully, I was already finished with the process of relieving myself as I dropped to the floor out of fear.

Witnesses recalled two individuals wearing in Halloween masks. The passenger doing the shooting had strong enough arms with "Only God Can Judge Me" in Old English written across his arm. Too bad that's a fairly standard description to incriminate anyone. The driver looked feminine with a white wig.

Matter of fact, I did remember that the driver of the early 90s Mustang 5.0 tearing off from the church parking lot had white hair like GangBang. *Wait!* She had to be with him during the shooting. I wonder why I never put this together sooner.

Funny how the entire hood came to pay my mother respect at the funeral, but none of them would help corroborate with the police. Then again, considering the cops I've run into, who would blame them?

Trekking across the posh suburb of South Barrington, I know the residence of Hollow Point is near. Cars from expensive dealerships are parked up and down the street. From my distance, all that's audible are the muffled sounds of a wild party and bass. The street ends at a cul-de-sac where Hollow Point's house looked like it was straight out of one of those old episodes I saw of MTV Cribs.

It seems like there are ton of people partying up inside. Two armed security men are posted by the gate, blocking off the driveway entrance to the home. Both were tall, linebacker looking niggas. Earpieces meant they were connected to other members of his personal security force inside. A tablet in each of their hands ensured only those chosen made it in.

"Can I help you, sir?" the baldheaded gentlemen said as he swayed purposely to display his Desert Eagle tucked into his waistband.

"Yo, I'm not on the guest list," I admit. "I'm just here to kill Hollow Point."

"The fuck you mean, nigga?" the same bouncer says, pulling out his Desert Eagle and his partner does the same. Both drop the tablets.

I have no real reason to kill them. They both seem like decent enough people who are just doing their job.

I raise my hands and play coy. My palms glow red as I knock them both to sleep. Dragging one man's hand to the hand scanner to open the gate, both shake as if they're having the worst nightmare of their life. Well, that's because they are.

The driveway weaves toward the front entrance featuring a large centered fountain. This is an event for ballers as the driveway is lined with Range Rovers, Maseratis, a Lamborghini Aventador, BMWs, and a few models of old school Detroit muscles. His front yard was worth more than the whole city he came from. I could see the glitz inside from the front double doors being wide open.

European art littered the marble hallway leading into the expansive foyer. The DJ was set up there pounding out the latest in popular music while sampling some of Hollow Point's first drafts for his upcoming mixtape. A nearby display made up of several flatscreen televisions flashed with his music videos. Females with beautiful bodies and faces lounged and strolled throughout the residence as if this was a lower scale Playboy Mansion.

There wasn't a soul who passed by me without a red cup in their hands filled with liquor. Puffs of smoke hung from guests blowing on the finest herb. Many were like zombies off the latest designer drug. There were a lot of doors. Another hallway leads into a state-of-the-art kitchen with two chefs stirring pots and a cute young server plating salmon canapes.

This was everything folks on social media and blogs would refer to as one of the wildest parties of the year. I looked over and saw a fairly famous model getting fucked doggy style on a wall without a care in the world. Both were going at it like they'd just taken the purest rail of cocaine. Can't lie, that was a bit of a turn-on.

Matter of fact, those sober enough to hold their phones straight took various selfies and snapped pics of the wild moments. These were going to be embarrassing episodes tomorrow if they lived.

"Where the fuck is Hollow Point?" I whispered to myself as I noticed a small crowd gathering nearby the pool house. The color show splashing the property and people pulsated to the heavy 808s sonically stomping throughout the entire compound. Empty bottles of top shelf spirits and expensive champagnes were strewn around the pool area awaiting more company.

I knew I was out of place in the environment, but those that might have noticed thought I was just the janitor or something to that effect. As I surveyed the scene discreetly, I formulated my plan. Rushing in and killing everyone including guests with no real ties to Hollow outside of whatever monetary gain they can make would be in bad taste. Instead, I had a better idea. In my peripherals was a half empty bottle of Hennessy sitting by itself on a small glass table near the pool. This is going to be fun.

As I grabbed the bottle, the DJ started playing the opening interlude to GangBang's debut EP on Hollow's label Rich Niggaz Entertainment titled "Creampie & Tech Nines." No music or rhyme on the first track, just him speaking the most disturbing monologue I've ever heard:

> College? For what? You take some bullshit classes, get all this debt and can't find no job afterwards. Your parents end up hating you and treating you like shit because you old and living in they house.

I say fuck that. What's the point? Look at this bitch. She's been my bottom bitch since we was doing drive-bys in the old school. Remember that, baby? She plays her position, which is what you gotta do to survive in this game. See now, don't nobody give a fuck about yo' problems or what you been through. I've been through some shit but I worked my way out and up. Figured how to turn my story into art. Now I got platinum hit after platinum hits and all you hoes trying to lick my ass trying to get chose. Cute shit, really.

See this bitch played her role perfectly and now gets a hand at my riches. Even got her a record deal. What's yo' name baby?

Then a few gunshot sound clips are followed by police sirens before GangBang spits the first verse of the titular track.

Real name Marsha Holmes, GangBang had been raised to do whatever was necessary to survive. Being molested the day before getting her first period created something inhuman. But who needed psychiatric counseling when one had Mount Ebal? Before turning 18, she was already a master at turning tricks. Her abusive pimp introduced her to Hollow Point, whom he received cocaine from. She later killed the man she once had to call daddy on the regular with a revolver given to her by the man who would influence her life the most.

I'd seen enough music videos to recognize his weed man Dizzy, who was passed out with a few hoes inside a canopy tent about a hundred feet away. None of them even looked up as I eased near. Pouring the remaining cognac on the cotton sofa, they didn't notice until the fire I set with my fingers became unavoidable.

"Oh shit! Fire! Damn, nigga!" he yells as everyone in the pool area rushes inside. The fire spreads to a nearby bush, hitting grass leading to the kitchen area of the home. Word spreads quickly before Hollow Point and everyone inside realizes a problem.

The bodyguards patrolling the outside rush inside as if to make sure Hollow is safe. Their real goal is to escape from the side gate. They fail to understand my power. It's locked and no one is leaving tonight. No one could call or use their cellphone as I had disabled the signals.

Hollow was smart enough to have a party this lit be under control as much as he could. Last year, he just beat a charge for having sex with a fourteen-year-old girl who snuck into the party last year. Despite video evidence through camera phone and eyewitnesses, the women in question didn't testify. After some media and public backlash, he'd drop one of the biggest singles of his career to date called "Slip It In" and all was forgiven, or at least, it was forgotten.

Too bad no one had cell phone reception to call the fire department. They were trapped. Hollow Point, GangBang, and the manager Ricky J thought it was another hater or possible longtime foe from the hood attempting to inflict revenge. He'd had a similar instance three years ago on his War tour. A heated argument over a rival rapper speaking to his side chick ended with his best friend Coz getting stabbed to death in the back of a gentlemen's club champagne room. 'Til this day, Coz's baby momma gets ten thousand a month from him. His irresponsibility killed Coz, leaving a family financially broken. He said his past couldn't allow that cycle to continue.

But considering what he did to my family, Hollow was a hypocrite. He couldn't let that happen again. They were ready and prepared as if they were going to war like years past. By then, word had spread around and everyone there realized it was me. Before I got to the broad shoulder ass niggas, a few of his homies from around the way attempted to unload several buckshots and bullets into me before I make their heads explode in a shower of gore and blood.

"Oh, fuck this!" a man screams as he runs to the front yard along with many of the party members. To my surprise, common sense prevailed. Everyone scattered like roaches. Busting down the poolhouse door wasn't hard and the panicked screams from the inside sounded like a bunch of little kids who come up on a snake. I force Hollow Point and GangBang to remain in their seats. The rest of his crew is easy work and with only a quick thought from my mind, they combust and only their burned flesh and smoking ash piles remain smoldering around the room.

I'm watching GangBang scream like a little kid as she sat motionless on the soft all white leather couch splattered with blood and other human chunks. Of course, watching her scream hysterically and beg for freedom only satisfied my hunger for redemption. Truthfully, my dick got hard.

But Hollow Point was still and calm, without emotion. Almost as if he welcomed his fate with open arms. Nothing I did would surprise him. Life made him cold enough to be unaffected on even a supernatural level. He watched his homies and trusted associates all explode around him without much care in the world. Families would be broken forever, homes shattered.

My other head was still erect and GangBang looked fine. Plus, she wouldn't shut the fuck up. Disconnecting her head from the spine was easy work for me. I dug my claws past the wig and weave to her short roots. For a firmer grip, I penetrated a piece of GangBang's fairly empty brain. The first tug broke her neck. The second disconnected her spine and tore flesh. The last one did it. It was redeeming watching the geyser of blood erupt from her neck down past her double-D cups.

Hollow Point was still unfazed but I knew I could break him. Placing GangBang's head into my left hand, I used my thumb to unzip my tattered jean zipper. Reaching through my boxers, I whip it out.

As my dick slipped through GangBang's mouth and exited at the bottom of her throat, I saw him break. The tears coming from his eyes served as a sweet notification. The wickedness of Hollow's past was turned back on him in flashes in his mind. Then again, watching his bottom bitch's skull around my dick didn't help either. I came pretty quick though, just like it was the first time. Guess one could say she gave me brain like NYU.

Feeling spent, I drop her useless head on the floor, plop down next to Hollow, and wrap my right arm around him as if we had been friends for decades. I smiled at him, then I got dead serious. "You know, you niggaz sure did know how to make someone's life a living hell; shooting up churches and shit," I said.

"I did whatever the fuck I had to do, nigga," Hollow retorts. "So you gon' get this over with and kill me?"

"Hold up for a sec. I wanna tell you about something I read on Wikipedia about the Anasazi people. Meaning 'ancient people' in the Navajo tongue, the Anasazi were masterful architects. Only a great people would understand the ways of Mother Nature enough to build beautiful living quarters on the sides of mountains and shit. You should look it up," I say to him.

He doesn't look at me, just keeps staring straight ahead.

"See, one of the things they were known for was eating their enemies once defeated." I pause.

Hollow Point still doesn't look at me, but I turn his chin so I can see his eyes as I say my last bit. "Sir, you have been defeated."

Those snakelike scales that had grown since days prior became even more prominent. My skin felt stronger yet looser. The world looked different. Bones began to crack and deform into something else. Teeth got sharper, claws sharper. A monstrosity not meant for human eyes to see, my frame doubled vertically and horizontally. Every piece of clothing I had on ripped clean off.

And there I am, a super demon. The total transformation only took a few seconds.

Ripping the rapper in half was easy. Swallowing that dead nigga was the hard part; he was still wiggling a bit. Had to wash that nigga down with a nearby bottle of Dom Perignon. Who knew human flesh and expensive champagne went so well together?

Epilogue

11 : 00PM

So now, after years of torment, everyone responsible for my parents' deaths were destroyed. But revenge cost me everything: my mind, my body, and remaining parts of my soul. Life became more exciting and purposeful, if only for three days. I'm already passed out in my room as the cops, ambulances, and fire trucks start to take in the scene back at Hollow Point's. They're going to have one hell of a night by the time they get back there. I doubt they'll even believe the eyewitness accounts. The shit was just too unreal.

Naked, hot, and alone, I knew what was next. The closet had that glow. My fate was sealed. Grabbing the barely alive netbook, I start recording. I introduce myself and get right to it.

Pay close attention to these words ladies and gentlemen; old and young.

The price was heavy for the deal I made with a particular fallen angel. By now, you understand that wasn't some metaphorical shit either. Those who don't know my story will ask questions regarding my decision. The only answer I can give them is to try playing a game like The Sims.

The Sims were created by this white dude, Will Wright, a master of design and philosophy. A game where the goal is to live alongside a virtual human; that's it. Very mundane, I'd say. Watching them go about their everyday business like working a bullshit 9-5 or cooking. They speak this chopped up slurred version of English called Simlish. Voyeurism doesn't get any creepier.

But the interesting thing is this: you can do some asshole shit like locking them in a house with a bunch of fireworks that will eventually kill them or type in "rosebud" and make them instantly rich. You have the power to make someone's life a living hell or one filled with infinite bliss. Quite an amazing experience, I must say. You get a firsthand look in to what it's like to be God because you are God, in theory.

Fascinating shit because that's how God works. He makes some folks rich and makes some folks poor or places someone in a house full of fireworks and expects them to be happy with their life. I guess my problem is that I refused to accept my fate.

I took matters into my own hands to destroy those who worked against me.

Those looking to be free from their bullshit existence know where to go. Facebook, Twitter, YouTube, and Soundcloud accounts explain my experience, available for anyone willing to listen.

Be warned, though! There are consequences to all actions committed in this story and the location was through that closet. It called for me, demanded my presence.

Considering the events, all I could do was oblige. Three days of infinite possibilities sounded like an easy trade off and solution, until you realize that the problems within my community will continue on, but with new faces.

Johnny D will be replaced at HD Chicken by the next one willing to be the next nigga at the slave plantation churning out fried delectables. Quesha would have been perfect if she hadn't quit the same night and decided to join the military. An assistant minister will just replace Pastor Jackson and continue to mentally fuck with the trusting and vulnerable community.

The prison industrial complex and local government my dad fought so hard to warn everyone of will create more unnecessary gang violence. Record labels will continue to exploit our pain and hunger to escape the hood. Another rapper will take the place of Hollow Point and GangBang. All it takes is someone with enough dope money to invest in themselves to produce a radio hit. And like before, people will listen and support the soundtrack to their own self-destruction in large numbers. And with so few educational and employment opportunities, it just means more criminals willing to risk it all robbing gas stations and convenience stores.

I tried to fight Satan with Satan and came up a bit short. That's what worrying about the puppets and not the puppeteer gets you. Time will inevitably move on as if nothing I did mattered.

Artificial? Yes, but hope came in a bottle of mayhem tonight.

I press stop on the recording and stand up.

I open the closet door to the same hellish view from before. My left foot hovers over the ledge. Tilting forward just a bit and I begin the descent to the unknown. As I tumble and fall down, down, down, I'm wondering and second-guessing my decision. *Should I have just let things be? Could life have gotten any better? Did I make the correct choice?* The fall gave me time to think and yet, it still wasn't enough.

That answer revealed itself to me in the best way possible as I splashed into the warm goo. Steady and floating on my backside, I saw more bodies falling.

As I drifted in the warm, welcoming fluid, I floated into a dark room with countless screams circling me like watching a horror flick on the best Dolby system money could buy. The small beam of light reveals the devil himself—well, herself, as a closer look reveals that same women who made me a man just days before.

But this time, the warm welcome isn't here. Chains appear from every direction and hold me in place. Flames engulf me as I'm forced to watch Granny, Mother, and Father enjoy the fruits of heaven in a panoramic view. All I can do is shake my head and crack a smile.

Ural Garrett is a journalist, photographer, and graduate of Southern University & A&M College. For the past several years, the Inglewood, California native has written for popular publications ranging from HipHopDX to Complex. This is his first published novel. Those looking to witness his various adventures can see what's up on his portfolio site: UralG.com.

more titles from

GRIEF AND NEW GRAVES
by Edward "Little Man" Lewis

SWEET PETER DEEDER
by Odie Hawkins

YOUNG LOCS ON THE WESTSIDE, PARTS I & II
by The Legendary Ali

GRIEF AND NEW GRAVES
by Edward "Little Man" Lewis

DEFINITION OF DOWN:
MY LIFE WITH ICE T & THE BIRTH OF HIP HOP
by Darlene Ortiz & Heidi Cuda

6 'N THE MORNING
by Daudi Abe

CHECK OUT EVEN MORE AT
OVERTHEEDGEBOOKS.COM

FOLLOW US ON IG & TWITTER
@OVERTHEEDGEBOOK